TRESTLE OVER NO NAME CREEK

Cheryl et al!
so grateful am I for
memories (10-years of youth camp
and my human
Linus blanket(s)

Marie C. Senter
Deut 33:25

TRESTLE OVER NO NAME CREEK

First in the
MARY CLARE & the Meanderthallers
Mystery Series

MARIE C. SENTER

Brenda Hussain
EDITOR

FRANKLIN
SCRIBES™

PUBLISHERS

Published by Franklin Scribes Publishers. Franklin Scribes is a registered trademark of Franklin Scribes Publishers.

Franklin Scribes books may be purchased in bulk for educational, business, fund-raising, or sales promotional use. For information, please email **SpecialMarkets@FranklinScribes.com**

Publisher's Note: This novel is a work of fiction. References to events, establishments, organizations, locales, and real people living or deceased are intended merely to equip the fiction with a sense of authenticity and color. They are used fictiously. All other names, characters, places, and all dialogue and incidents portrayed in this book are the product of the author's imagination.

Senter, Marie C.
TRESTLE OVER NO NAME CREEK / Marie C. Senter

Summary: Frank, a dark-skinned old man, is found dead in No Name Creek under the railroad trestle. The local small town kids unravel the mysteries surrounding the old man they called "Friend." In the 1960's, the idea of a friend over 30, a grown-up they could call by first name, a friend with no last name who liked to visit and teach them interesting stuff was reactionary—and now he was dead! The grown-ups ignored him. No one knew or cared who he was except the kids. Surviving life controlled by rigid codes of conduct, every move monitored by grown-ups (and the local tattle-tale cop), the junior high kids gather in the back booth of the local Drug Store 'n Soda Fountain Shop after school to share accumulated clues. They form the Meanderthaller gang and set out to uncover the truth. Was Frank's death an accident, as the grown-ups prefer to think, or was Frank's death a murder?

ISBN 978-0-9886433-4-5 (soft cover)

Printed in the United States of America

DEDICATION

This book is dedicated to teachers: people who take time to share knowledge, encourage, challenge, and inspire. They are individuals who, by example, show how study, patience, determination, and plain ol' never-quit-itis can make a difference.

Mostly, this book is dedicated to that "still, small voice" within each that will lead us truly if we wait, have faith, and believe in the talents we are given.

Chapter 1

FRANK'S FRIENDS

"Frank is missing!" Janie slid into the back booth of the Soda Fountain Shop and grabbed her brother's root beer float. "Frank's missing!" She repeated after a slurp of the float.

"Gimme my float back!" Janie nudged the float toward her brother Donnie. I slapped the top of the booth table before a brother-sister squabble could take off.

"Janie! Donnie! Stop it! Now, what's this 'Frank missing' bulletin?"

Janie let go of the float. "Frank is free as a bird to come and go, but Ma went up to check his room after he missed supper last night, breakfast this morning, and now lunch."

Us junior high girls giggled, and the boys snorted at the thought of Frank missing a chance to eat. Meals are the only thing Frank has on his schedule.

A sharp elbow dug into my rib cage, and Melvin, the city kid import to our small town, asked, "Who's Frank?"

We all answered at the same time, and Melvin learned. "Frank is our friend."

"He's an old old man who teaches us stuff—just because."

"My pop says he's older than dirt and just as dark."

"His skin looks dark, like bad sunburn, not dirt."

"My gramps says he wandered into town and never left."

"Grown-ups don't pick on him. They ignore him."

"We adopted him—or maybe, he adopted us."

"We sometimes meet him where the trestle crosses No Name Creek."

Melvin's eyes glazed over. "Whoa! Slow down! Do you guys practice talking alike? You sound like a chorus when you talk all at once. I'll say, it takes some getting used to." He jabbed a straw into a Nehi Orange and took a slurp. "You guys actually have a grown-up for a friend? 'n you call him by his first name? My papa would blister my behind if I called a grown-up by his first name. What's the rest of his name? Where's he from? Who is he?"

We looked at Melvin, then at each other in total astonishment. Not one of us could remember if we had ever asked Frank those questions. In our world, asking such questions would earn a swat for being nosy, followed by somebody telling us to "mind our own beeswax!" Plus, if we didn't ask *them* nosy questions, then it wouldn't be mannerly for *them* to ask *us*. Respect for privacy acts like a closed door between folks—with no latch to open it without an invitation.

I think that's when we realized how much we took Frank's friendship for granted. For Melvin's benefit, I put words to thought, "Frank has always been around, so we expect him to always be around. He's not like most grown-ups; mostly, we're treated like we're dumber than a fence post."

Little C, my sister, yelped, "Not Frank! He treats us like val-a-ble hooman beans who deserve…deserve…"

"…respect!" Janie banged her empty mug down, "and he likes teaching us stuff."

Little C kept talking, "'n he doesn't mind if we forget and hafta' ask him to repeat what he taught us last time."

Melvin nodded, and then he made a mental right turn, "Somebody tell me: what is a trestle?"

Kay, the preacher's daughter, our grammar-and-word-use warden, volunteered, "The correct name for that tall wood bridge that carries trains across No Name Creek is *trestle*."

But Little C wasn't through with her thought, "…'n Frank likes to stop and teach us stuff like names for rocks he has in his pockets."

Melvin lit up, "Rocks? I can make a rock skip seven times on water. It's gotta be a flat rock about the size of my hand—er—the palm of my hand."

I whistled in awe, "Seven times! I'm impressed. But the rocks Frank carries are usually too little for throwing, 'n they're all shapes."

"Does he keep them for pets? Do little rocks have the same names as big rocks?"

"I don't know if he has pet rocks, but he knows all their names," I said, "Mostly, I think Frank likes talking to us. He tells us it's okay to ask him questions we wouldn't ask any other grown-up, like why does he go walking alone when he could be having donuts and coffee with the other old folks? Or, is his skin that dark color all over?"

"Maybe being in the sun so much is what made his skin so dark." Janie slipped that in and followed with, "He thanked me for the bar of my gram's lye soap, but it didn't wash any of that dark color away."

"My ma has warned me to stay out of the sun 'cause my skin might stay dark." Donnie showed us the still-white skin under his shirt sleeve. "I didn't believe her until I saw how dark Frank's skin stays even in winter."

"An old man with dark skin sounds like a …shucks, I can't say that word—it ain't a nice word. Hey! Have you small town kids ever seen a negro—a black man?" Melvin had us wide eyed and momentarily speechless. With one voice we answered that Frank looked permanently, darkly, sun tanned, not black.

"And Frank is the only grown-up we call using one name…"

"Mary Clare, you tell the story, but wait till we order another round."

Okay. Now I can fill in some blanks while EJ, my brother, goes up to the Soda Fountain and gets Mr. Murrey started on some Green Mountains or Nehi Orange or Barg's Root Beer Floats or Coke Floats or whatever. I am the self appointed leader of this group of junior high kids from in town. We can get together after school here in the back booth of the Drug Store Soda Fountain if we buy something and don't get rowdy.

"Quit talking to yourself, Mary Clare. Tell Melvin how we got to callin' Mr. Frank just Frank."

"It's all because I go exploring by myself, which is okay as long as I tell my mom which way I'm going exploring. You need to know Frank does a lot of walking by himself, too."

"I bet he doesn't have to check in with anyone or tell anyone where he is going or when, does he?" Melvin is new in town and doesn't realize every grown-up looks out for every kid all the time here.

"You're right about Frank not needing to check in, and that's sad 'cause none of the grown-ups notice, or care. I think we kids are his only friends. Let me tell you how the Frank-for-a-friend story starts. The other side of the railroad right-of-way fence is my grandparents' back yard. Some critter had dug a hole under the wire mesh. We kids enlarged the hole so we could sit on our jeans bottoms, slide down the tunnel through the tall weeds, set our heels just before we hit the railroad grade ditch full of icky water, stand up and jump the ditch Walla! Railroad tracks to the trestle.

"The right word is *voila*. That's French for *bingo*!" Kay, the preacher's daughter, was always correcting our vocabulary.

We ignored her 'cause we were giggling remembering the times we missed setting our heels, and we'd end up in the icky, stinky water. Yuck!

"Anyways, one time I almost collided with Frank as I jumped the ditch. I've heard him tell his version of our near collision. 'I was walking the tracks, minding my own business, when this little girl with pig-tail braids came h-e-double-fence-post bent for heaven into my life.'"

"H-e-double-fence-post is the non-swearing way to say *hell*." explained Kay.

"Anyways, I stuck out my hand, introduced myself using proper manners my mom would have been proud of, and he shook my hand and said, 'Call me Frank.' My eyes went from the wavy grey/black hair, the cool-blue eyes, the too-white-to-be-real teeth, the clean denim shirt, the pressed khaki pants and sturdy walking boots holding him steady on the railroad grade."

"Tell Melvin about the heart dangling from his pocket watch chain!"

"A heart? A real heart?" Melvin was almost stuttering in excitement. "What color is a heart? I hear a real heart isn't really blood red. How did he have it tied to his chain?"

"It was a goldstone heart. That's a semi-precious gem stone. Frank said it was a gift from a fellow scoundrel."

"A what? A skow…skun…whaducall it?"

Little C, my little sister, piped up to explain, "Goldstone is sorta kinda red. Mary Clare can't see colors right, but Frank's watch fob is a copper-red goldstone."

"Anyways, EJ, my brother, came sliding down the tall-weed tunnel, and jumped the ditch as Frank and I were introducing ourselves."

"Yeah," EJ put in, "Mary Clare is telling it like it happened. I called him Mr. Frank, and he asked me to call him plain, ol' Frank. I invited him to come check the catch-pool fish traps under the trestle. He said thank you, but he didn't want to come just then. Then he offered to teach us kids about rocks 'n stuff anytime we liked."

Melvin pulled out a flat, sparkly stone and showed us where someone had painted the name Rocky on it. "This has been my pet rock since I was a little kid, and pet rocks were a big thing. I still have it 'cause it reminds me of some fun times I had with my folks."

"That looks like a piece of granite with all those sparklies."

"Yeah. Flint would be solid grey."

"Frank has agates, shale—"

"Hey, squirts!" The gruff voice from over our heads scattered our chitter-chatter. "Hey, you kids. Where's your friend, Mr. Frank?" We sat stunned into silence as Ronnie B, the biggest kid in high school, stood looking down on us lowly junior-high kids. "That old man hasn't been to football practice for days, and there's a big game coming up."

I looked around at my speechless classmates. All I saw were big eyes and open mouths that couldn't get words out—except for Melvin.

"What do you big, scary football players want with an old man?"

Ronnie B ignored Melvin's question. Maybe Melvin's high-pitched voice didn't register against Ronnie B's ear drums, or maybe he didn't want to answer a junior high kid's question, but he answered anyway. "Us guys like havin' that old man watch. He's like a good-luck charm. The team told me to find him. I figured if anybody knew where he was, you squirts would know."

My gloved hand clamped over Melvin's mouth. I regained my voice and coughed up the news about Frank missing meals at the Komfy Kozy Kave-inn.

Janie added, "He hasn't been in his room for a couple days." The chorus chimed in with promises to search the town and some of our favorite places out in the country.

Ronnie B growled, "Thanks! Let me know!" The wooden floor of the Soda Fountain shook as he rumbled away. Wow! This was serious. Frank was the one grown-up who took time to listen to us kids, and he never treated us like we were dumber than a fence post.

Before I could say anything, Melvin got going. "Whoever that big overgrown hulk is, he needs to learn manners. Next time, I'm not going to let him stomp all over us—er—you guys."

He looked at the stunned-into-silence chorus facing him, and then he hung a verbal right turn, "I told you that if I ever called an old guy by his first name, my papa would blister my behind, and I ain't never heard of havin' anybody over thirty for an actual, real friend."

"Cork it! Dad just walked in the door!" EJ slipped back into the booth.

"Quick! Grab a pencil and make like we're doin' homework!" My face was almost touching the paper when Dad walked by on his way to the pay phone. He paused, and I know he was looking right at me, but he walked on. I heard the dime click into the phone before he slid the phone booth door closed.

"Gee whiz, Mary Clare! Why are you so spooked by your Dad?" Melvin, being the new kid, didn't know the history, and I couldn't think of a quick answer. "Mary Clare, you act like you don't love your father or he doesn't love you. What's the matter?"

We sat with our mouths open at these nosy questions.

"Does he spank you? Don't 'cha know Dad's got spanked when they were kids for doing something wrong, so they spank us for doing something they see as wrong."

Our voices collided responding.

"Hey, city kid, we ain't totally igner'nt."

"We get spanked."

"But by hand, not with a belt."

"Or with a switch, like my Ma got willow-switched when she was a kid"

"But words hurt just as much…"

"or more 'cause of bein' a disappointment…"

"or always bein' wrong 'n not getting to 'splain…

"Ya know, sometimes, mostly, being a kid is a pain."

"Maybe it's different in a big city."

"Anyways, city kid, it ain't none of your beeswax."

Melvin was sitting there trying to get a word in edgewise, and I bet my face was beet-red from embarrassment. Melvin made a sudden mental right turn and bailed me out.

Okay! Okay! Forget I asked. Mainly, I want to join in the hunt for Frank. I feel like I already know him.

A chorus sigh was the answer, and we quickly assigned areas to check out in the morning.

I heard the door to the phone booth slide open as we scooted out of the booth heading for the front door. It was just about supper time, so we reminded each other to keep a sharp look out for Frank as we headed home.

"And pass the word when you find him..."

"...Or he finds us!"

EJ and I took the short cut home to stay ahead of dad. As we jogged, Melvin's question circled in my brain. How do I find out if my dad likes me for a daughter? Or, even more of a challenge, how do I figure out if he loves me?

Chapter Two

HUNTING FOR FRANK

It had snowed overnight, so there was a covering of that cold, white stuff to crunch 'n stomp through in the morning.

"C'mon, Mary Clare. Move it! Grab your gloves for those precious hands of yours, and let's go find Frank." EJ was ready as usual, and I was still trying to get it together. We wore three buckle overshoes, flannel jackets, earmuffs, and jersey gloves over our regular clothes as we started out to find Frank. Mom wanted to know what we planned to do with a Saturday, so I told her us town kids were gonna turn the town upside down looking for Frank. EJ was as excited as I was, and both of the dogs were whining and jumping around. Dad heard us, and when EJ said we were going to search for Frank around the trestle, Dad gave us an early Christmas present.

"I cleaned the .410 shotgun last night, so EJ, take the gun, and you two bring back some of those cottontails who got fat feasting on Gran'ma Asklund's garden all year!"

Wow! What a present! EJ looked at me, and I looked at EJ without saying the words we both were thinking. Dad had spent a lifetime teaching us gun safety. He showed us by letting us go along on pheasant hunting trips, and then we got BB guns so we could practice shooting. We were to receive our choice of shotgun for high school graduation present, but EJ, being the oldest son, got to use a real shotgun way before he was even in high school. The gun was a .410 hammer action, single shot: the closest thing to an accident-proof shotgun there is.

I guess it hadn't hit me that I didn't have a shotgun until just then. I'm older than EJ, but I'm a girl, and Dad doesn't know what to do with me and my older sister. I saw the look on Mom's face and knew a .410 would be arriving for me immediately—soon—post haste—well, maybe. If I said anything now, it would ruin the day. That was just the facts, man, so today EJ will be able to bring back rabbits as we hunt for Frank. I grinned back at EJ as he carefully put extra shells in his jacket pocket leaving one in the palm of his glove for quick access. How often we had heard, "Don't load the gun until you're in the field." What a special day this was going to be—hunting for Frank and rabbits.

We headed down the tracks with the dogs working the ditch for rabbits and the two of us looking for Frank. "There he is!" EJ pointed at a man climbing the railroad ditch.

"No. That's old Gram'pa Asklund. He's taller than Frank and doesn't wear a cap." I was so sure we would see Frank; I just knew I wouldn't have to resolve a dilemma. In my head I heard: "Dilemma! Mary Clare, you use the weirdest words!" The group was always teasing me about being a book worm. "You can't see to read the blackboard, but you see enough to read the weirdest books, and look up words nobody but you ever uses."

If Frank didn't appear, I would have to show Frank's hideout cabin to EJ. I stumbled across it on one of my walks in the old north timber/gravel pit, and I don't know if Frank knows I know it's there. It's so hidden; I never said anything or looked closer 'cause I respected his privacy! I never told anyone I knew about it, but if Frank didn't show up by the time we reached the trestle, I would go look in the cabin for Frank—with EJ. What a dilemma! "C'mon Frank. Make with the visibility!"

EJ looked at me and said, "Huh?"

That's when I realized I had been talking to myself—again—and must have muttered out loud the request for Frank to show up. Anyways, we reached the trestle and No Name Creek without seeing any rabbits or catching a glimpse of Frank. "Reckafrex! Mom is going to make rabbit stew with carrots and potatoes and onions, and it would do Frank good to eat a bowl of it if we could get him to come for supper." EJ was rubbing his tummy as I described Mom's "stewp"—that's stew too thin to fork, and soup too thick to spoon. I sighed, "Well, let's cross the trestle and head for the north gravel pit. He might be there."

Cindy, our Black Labrador, followed us across the trestle. She didn't like the height with all that open space between the ties. No Name Creek could be seen way down there, and we were focused and quiet as we walked across. It was cold, windy, and the trestle felt slippery under my boots. I wondered if EJ was holding his breath like

I was. One slip would result in a bad sprained ankle, and a fall over the edge would be flat-out deadly. The creek was perfect for wading but too shallow for swimming, and you'd have to be crazy to try diving from the trestle.

Wags, my Chesapeake Bay retriever, would never have anything to do with the trestle. She would whine, jump around, and finally charge down the grade, splash across No Name Creek, scramble up the far side, and be waiting, with a silly grin on her face, for us to "get off that dangerous thing." This time, she was still down in the creek and would not come when we whistled and called. She was pulling on something in the creek under the trestle. Cindy went to investigate, and then neither one would answer our calls and whistles.

EJ looked at me, and I looked at him. Then he asked, "What are they trying to drag out of the creek?" Never before had the dogs ignored our whistles or calls. EJ carefully laid the .410 shotgun on the packed snow before we slid down the grade to the creek.

It was Frank. I almost got sick on the spot, and EJ let out a "NO!" scream. The dogs were trying to drag Frank out of the water. He was soaked through, and he was dead—really, truly, for-sure dead. The four of us pulled him up on the bank out of the water. Both the dogs put their tails between their legs and started whining; it sounded like they were crying. Cindy licked Frank's face and then curled up beside him. I pulled one of Dad's old handkerchiefs out of my back pocket and handed it to EJ so he could wipe his nose and dry the tears running down his face. I felt sick, scared, and shocked all at once. I wanted to cry, too, but I wasn't the kind to do that, so I sat down next to Frank and held his hand.

"Please, EJ, run back to town and get a grown-up to come, Doc Bucky, the policeman, Mr. LaFloy, or anyone who will come and take charge."

EJ kinda' gulped, blew his nose, and seemed glad to have something to do. I could barely understand his squeaky, whisper voice, "I'm scared. This is spooky. I'll go as fast as I can." He started running, slowed to a careful walk on the trestle, and then took off running again.

It was right that I stay with our dead friend until help could come. I didn't tell EJ to look for Dad 'cause I knew Dad was getting ready for work. I just didn't want Frank to be alone. I started talking to myself so I wouldn't feel so awful alone—with my dead friend. I believed in heaven, but I didn't know if he knew there was a place to go after you're dead. We had never talked about stuff like that; somewhere between him being old and me being young, we missed talking about death and what comes next. I let go of his cold hand when it started to make my hand cold. My glove was still warm so I pulled it on, but I kept shivering all over. The dogs and I huddled up keeping each other warm and, I'll be honest, their whining sounded so much like crying, I joined them. No one was there to see me, so I thought it would be okay. In my head, I could hear Cousin Ange. She always told me I was too much brain and not enough little girl.

"Gobs of Gramma's greasy gravy!" popped out of me when EJ arrived with a passel of the grown-ups dragging a stretcher. The town didn't have an ambulance, so they used the funeral home hearse. It couldn't get anywheres near, so the men had to carry and drag the stretcher a half-mile along the tracks and then skid down the grade to the No Name Creek bank where Frank lay. The town cop—er—policeman acted like he was in charge. Everyone agreed: Frank was dead, but it wasn't official until Doc Bucky said so. He slid to a stop just before he would have landed in the creek. He didn't even need his stethoscope. One look and a pat on Frank's cold face did it. Doc Bucky pronounced Frank officially dead. The men started pulling and pushing the stretcher over to where Frank's body was. EJ and I got out of the way and answered their questions about why we were there and how we knew Frank was here.

We sorta kinda took turns bouncing answers to questions. "Yesterday, we found out Frank was missing."

"Folks in town don't pay him no never mind, so nobody missed him."

"He hadn't been in his room or been to meals at the Komfy Kozy Kave-inn for a couple days, so we kids decided to find him."

"EJ and I chose this area to look for Frank, and we combined the search with a rabbit hunting trip."

"Wags won't cross the trestle, so she is the one who found Frank."

"We just dragged him onto dry land." We pointed out where his body had been, where his arms were stretched out like he had tried to fly, and I showed Doc Bucky the rock with blood on it where Frank's head had been. It was one of the big rocks we kids had dumped when we were trying to build a hop-scotch bridge. I got the shivers just thinking about it having Frank's blood on it, maybe right where our hands had been.

"Okay, kids, good job!"

"Very nice work!"

"You did everything right!"

That last came from Doc Bucky, and all the men chorused, "You bet! Cool thinking." It almost choked me up, and I was scared I would start crying in front of them. I was glad when someone looked up—way up—at the trestle high overhead.

The policeman said what everyone was thinking: "No one could live through a fall from that height."

That's when it hit me. These grown-ups were thinking this was an accident. It just didn't feel right to me. No way would Frank accidentally fall off our trestle. Somebody had to have pushed Frank or done something to cause this fall. This was a murder case. Period.

"Please, wait a minute. Frank always wore fur-lined leather gloves. Where are his gloves?"

Doc Bucky surprised me by adding, "His hands were to him what Samson's hair was to Samson. He took as good a care of his hands as I do mine."

The men looked at Doc Bucky, me, then at Frank's bare hands, then back at me before they shrugged their shoulders. It was getting colder by the minute, so I can understand why everyone took the quick and easy way out. The grown-ups decided old man Frank must have stumbled and fallen by accident.

"I guess we should bring the bloody rock for evidence." The cop—policeman—finally said something smart.

Little C wasn't there to pull my braid, so my mouth opened and out blurted, "Why do you need evidence if this was an accident?"

The policeman looked like I did when my dad caught me in a "situation." His growled "Shut your mouth!" startled the men, and they quickly got the policeman busy lifting the stretcher.

Doc Bucky carefully tucked the rock with the bloody side up in his doctor bag. He volunteered to check the surface of the trestle for ice. If there was ice, the grown-ups could blame the fall on the slippery surface of the trestle plus the cold wind plus Frank was an old man. EJ and I listened to them throw the topic back and forth until the consensus was: accidental death from an accidental fall.

They lifted Frank's body onto the stretcher, wrapped and strapped the body down, then roped-dragged-skidded it up the grade.

One more time, EJ and I looked over the creek where we had spent so much time fishing, wading, and just having fun. Something twinkled in the Creek where Frank's body had been. In a flash, I slid down the bank, bent down, put my bare hand in the ice-cold water, and picked up half of a goldstone heart twinkling in the No Name Creek water. Half a heart! Where was the other half? Was it Frank's watch-fob goldstone heart? I put it in my jacket pocket, pulled my glove back on, and turned to see what EJ was doing.

"Frank's cap—the one with the fur-lined ear flaps. Did you see his cap?" EJ had a completely reasonable answer to his own question. "Those ear flaps would have made it sail. If it had fallen in the creek, it would have drifted on the current until it got soaked, and then it would have sunk."

I just hate it when he's right 'cause that means I'm wrong, which means I should forget the missing cap, which doesn't satisfy me at all. We scrambled up the bank, picked up the gun, called the dogs, and that's when we realized we were on the far side of the trestle. Too much! I just couldn't handle Wags having to run down to the creek, splash across, and then scramble up the far side after all that had happened.

"Kids, you've had quite a day." Doc Bucky had checked the icy surface of the trestle and was waiting for us. "Come get in my car, and I'll take you home."

It was tempting, but I could just see the mess wet dogs would make in his big, fancy car. "Thank you, Doc Bucky, but it's just as close if we walk the tracks from here."

He just stood there, watching my face, waiting for me to say more.

"Sir, Mom and Dad are scheduled to play for a dance at The Cobblestone Ballroom tonight, and they need to get going. Could you please drive by the house and…?"

Doc Bucky studied us a minute. He promised to get to our home first and tell our folks what had happened. Doc Bucky telling them and letting them know we were okay would free up everybody to get on with living-as-usual. Nothing could be done about Frank, we were not injured, and the job at The Cobblestone was bread and butter for the family. I could hear my dad saying: "There's no need to get mushy, even with a good excuse—er—reason."

EJ and I watched as Doc Bucky double timed the tracks to his car. EJ picked up Wags to carry her across the trestle. I carried the .410 and Cindy followed us very carefully. Once we cleared the trestle, we hot-footed it for home, and when we turned the final corner, the car was gone, which meant mom and dad had gone on to the job. EJ and I looked at each other in relief. His eyes were still red and puffy from crying, but he hadn't cried since we left Doc Bucky. If the folks had been waiting, we both might'a broke down and started crying like the kids we were.

I was so busy being busy, it hadn't really hit me that our friend Frank wouldn't be meeting us and teaching us stuff ever again. Janie was right about Frank being missing—dead right.

Chapter Three

THE MEANDERTHALLERS

"Gee whiz, I'm sure sorry to hear about Frank." Melvin looked like he really was sorry. "Now tell me all about it. Was he bad smashed up from the fall? Was there a lot of blood? Did you get sick just lookin'? Was he all stiff when the men loaded him on the stretcher?"

"Stop! Stop it! The only way I can handle Frank's death is to not think about it, so zip your lip!" My face must have shown my feelings.

"Okay, okay." Melvin did a u-turn and started over, "I wanna' thank you for letting me join in the search. And what do I have to do to join this gang?"

"Gang! What a word to call us!" The chorus hissed in disapproval. Melvin looked surprised at our reaction to the word *gang*.

"It was a couple three weeks ago," Anne D explained. "I heard a lavender-haired old lady muttering about a gang of kids on their bikes getting her yappy little yard dog all excited. She called us a gang! Crickety! That little dog wanted to get out of that yard and go with us. I'd bark, too if I had to stay inside a fence, but why would she call us a gang?"

"A gang! I can hear the music to *West Side Story* right now! Remember the dance routine those guys did on the basketball court?" Nancy, our actress-in-training, started waving her arms in the air.

As I ducked, I explained, "The big dictionary in the library has a lotta' stuff about gangs. None of the definitions fits us. For sure, we aren't a band of juvenile delinquents."

Melvin looked like he was listening but still not getting it.

"We are a group of small-town kids, not law breaking juvenile delinquents! We're usually together and everybody in town knows us. The farm kids belong to FFA or 4H and have fancy jackets 'n stuff with their special club names. They are club members, not gangs. It's time we had a name for us town kids." I pounded on the booth top. "Names! A name everybody in town will hear and know who—whose name it is."

"I vote for Mosby Raiders! We're studying about the Grey Ghost, the name given Confederate Colonel Mosby, and his cavalry troops earned the name "Mosby Raiders." I vote we call ourselves the Mosby Raiders!" Anne D had a horse, so it made sense that she would want to name a group after some horse riders.

The chorus groaned and made some negative noises.

"Mary Clare, you are the leader, why don't you come up with a name for us?" Nancy put me on the spot. Before I could answer, my little sister spoke up.

"How about the...meander...meander-thall...ME-AN-DER-THALL-ERS!"

We looked at each other, remembering the stories about the Neanderthals, prehistoric man wandering/meandering around. With one voice, the chorus shouted, "YES," and just like that, we sixth-and-seventh-grade town kids became a named group—well, gang!

I gave my little sister a quick hug, something I just don't do, but I was so proud of her. Little C has trouble saying some words with *l*'s and *m*'s, and she gets teased for saying "arumamum" instead of "aluminum." Meanderthaller has *m*'s, *n*'s, and *l*'s, and she could say it clearly.

"Meanderthal, not Neanderthal. Neanderthal is ancient. Meanderthal is the today-way-to-GO! MEANDERTHALLERS! Yeah!" The chorus was on a roll.

"Wait till the farm kids hear what a cool name we have!"

"Wow! Can I be a charter member? This will be the first do-good-gang I ever heard of!" Melvin was so excited he bumped over his almost-empty root beer mug. Everybody grabbed a napkin and mopped up the spill before it could turn into a mess. It made me realize how much we had learned about getting along and working through problems, just hanging out together after school. Sure, we could get into trouble, but we were not law-breakers.

Melvin continued, "I almost fell into a real gang 'cause they had their own tee shirts and hand signals, almost like their own society, and it sure sounded good until my papa sat me down in the front room of our house—that front room was for special company only, so I knew something was up. He put me in the guest chair, pulled up an ottoman..."

The chorus took off, "A what?"

"My ma won't let me use a word like that."

"Wasn't that a bunch of Arabs fighting the crusaders?"

"If you mean foot stool, say foot stool."

"C'mon, use American!"

Melvin held up his hand and kept going, "My papa went nose-to-nose with me and gave me a tour of what life as a real gang member would be like. He can whup up on any one guy, but a gang—a gang fights dirty. And they use baseball bats. Then he told me I was going to disappear for the rest of the school year. He actually had tears in his eyes when he told me they love me enough to send me away to safety. If that doesn't register as love, you guys really do not know what love is."

We coughed, sneezed, grabbed for napkins and otherwise dodged that loaded word. Love was our parents approving/disapproving a movie before we could go. Love was what made the older kids get absolutely loopy. Love was for married folks, but love between parents and their kids was thin ice on a warm day. Mostly, we would talk about anything else unless one of us got a spankin' followed by "You're getting' a spanking 'cause I love you," and "This hurts me more than it hurts you." Then we might try to figure out what sense that made.

"My dad's never told me he loves me," It was out before I realized I was thinking out loud again. "I'm supposed to know 'cause he pays money for me to go to school, and there's always food to eat, 'n there's baseball bats, 'n I get my brother's old glove."

"Don't knock yourself, Mary Clare. My Pa says your dad brags about that home run you hit over the fence at Arny's Park. Didn't your dad give you a hug or at least pat your back, or somethin'?"

"Huh-uh. He was too busy tellin' EJ how to pitch to that kid who crowds the plate, but I've got that home run ball."

"No way, Jose! That ball sailed over the fence and into the tall weeds of the gully." With one voice, the chorus chorused, "It was Frank, wasn't it?"

"Yeah. Frank saw the hit, and after everybody left, he looked for that ball until dark. He was back at dawn and looked until he found it." I pulled a Melvin and right-turned into another subject.

"Does Mr. Tattle-tale policeman know about love? We kids don't even think about breaking rules. We even try to guess ahead and avoid what might get his attention 'cause we know he will run right to our parents, and we'll get double discipline for doin' whatever. That fact is a great motivator for good behavior." I shrugged, "It would be great if our dad's gave us kids credit for doin' something good. We sure hear about the stuff we don't do like they want. I don't think I'll ever hear the word *reason* without hearing my dad's voice: "There's no reason for doing it your way. That is an excuse for not doing it my way."

"You guys live lookin' over your shoulders—like you're expecting somebody to yell at you." We gawked as Melvin shared, "Where I came from, there were real gangs—gangs with tough people doing bad things—things a lot worse than yelling at you. There was one gang trying to requi...rekru...draft me. My folks sent me to live with my uncle Roy Witerok till things settle down." He blew his nose and kinda whispered, "I miss my folks. Maybe they can come visit this summer. I'd love to see 'em."

The Meanderthallers wiggled and shifted trying to handle such honest sharing. In the silence, I saw a light bulb go on in Melvin's brain. "Hey! I bet'cha Uncle Roy would let us have meetings in his big ol' ice house as long as we stay off the old straw-covered blocks of lake-ice."

"And we wouldn't have to be on the lookout for our dads." I blurted.

The chorus let out a whoop. "Great! We can still use the back booth at the Murrey Drug Store and Soda Fountain Shop as long as we buy something from Gran'pa Murrey—and look out for our dads!" We all started calling out the name of a favorite "something" to drink: "Green Mountain!"

"Nehi Orange!"

"Barg's Root Beer."

"Coke Float."

"Naw! Root Beer float is the best."

"Nope! The best is a double-chocolate malt." We agreed Gran'pa Murrey could make the absolute, most incredible, chocolate malt in the whole world, but in the ice house we wouldn't risk having somebody's dad break up our meeting just by walking in.

"Melvin, do you know how to play Capture the Flag?" Janie piped up. "You can join us next time. We're tough to beat 'cause we wear dark clothes, work together, and the bigger kids forget where we littler kids disappeared in the grass until one of us shows up in the ring with the flag-rag."

"Remember when the big kids got so mad I ran for home with the flag rag to escape." Elizabeth was so small and so quick she usually ended up with the flag. "I didn't want to stick around to see just how mad they got!"

Donnie let out a big "Ha!" followed by "I saw the big guys chasing you, then a pile-up of 'em. They said Frank stepped outta' the dark and tripped the lead chaser."

"That sounds like Frank. He was always there for us." Everybody took a quick sip so they wouldn't start crying. "How many times have we heard some grown-up say: 'kids should be seen, not heard'?" Heads bobbed up and down. "I guess they don't want to listen to the good questions we ask. It's easier to pay us no never mind than figure where Frank's gloves are. I can still feel his cold hands." I shivered at the memory.

"Mary Clare, give it up!" The chorus was worried I was too stuck on this clue.

"Okay, I'll quit talking about the missing gloves, but promise that each of us will listen and share overheard news, gossip, and clues. We are going to stay on this until the truth is clear."

I'll never forget the meeting a few days later when we each had something to share about goldstone hearts. Up until that meeting, I thought Frank had the only goldstone heart, which reminds me, I never did look up *scoundrel*. It was a scoundrel who gave Frank that goldstone heart on his pocket watch chain.

Anyways, Donnie said, "My pa has a goldstone heart, and it came with membership in the KKK."

"No! No! Say it isn't so! The KKK? Isn't that the bunch that wears those peaky hats and sheets with eye holes cut out, and they kill black people and they burn crosses?" I was talking so fast I almost bit my tongue. "The KluKluxKlan is not a nice group—er—gang—er—clan. Do you think the real KKK could even exist in our small town? And what would they be doing with goldstone watch fobs?"

"No! No! No!" Donnie was quick to redirect me, "My pa wears his goldstone heart as a member of the Kay Kayser Klub!"

"The who?" came as a chorus from the Meanderthallers.

"The Kay Kayser band was an orchestra that played for dances when our folks were young. I've heard my pa talk about driving to Sioux City to the Tamba Ballroom just to hear them. He got to go with his folks to see Kay Kayser in person. It was a big deal back then," Donnie shrugged and kinda grinned.

"Music! Dance music?" again from the Meanderthaller chorus.

"Yeah, my folks love to dance." Donnie continued. "They usually find a dance to go to on Saturday nights with a local music group playing, and everybody shows off new steps and routines. Everyone wears their goldstone heart to show who is a member of the KKK. It is possible some of your parents are dancers, too."

"Where did the members get goldstone hearts?" I was stunned to hear several of the Meanderthallers say, "Frank!"

"Frank gave my folks goldstone hearts."

"My mom put hers on a gold chain she wears around her neck."

"My papa put his on a tie tack."

"One little thing," I inserted, "If Frank is the source of goldstone hearts, can you see Frank dancing? Connecting Frank with dance music and dancing just didn't click. It's all I can do to watch my folks holding on to each other dancing. Yuck!"

"Yuck is right! That is sooooo—Kay, what word fits there?" Even Kay was wordless.

JR bailed outa the booth and started doing some weird jumping around. "Not all of it is yuck. My mother showed me a dance she learned as a kid called the Charleston, and I mean; I would love to be able to move like that!"

"Quit it! Quit it. Focus on Frank and the true story of the goldstone hearts. Robert, why is your hand up?"

"You're all wrong. If you knew all the guys in this town who have a goldstone heart, you would see they are all old high school sports heroes. Anyways, KKK stands for Knuckles, Knees 'n Koncussions."

Kay let out a yelp. "*Concussion* is correctly spelled with a *c*, never a *k*."

Robert had the answer ready. "Remember, these are football players, not spelling contestants, and concussion sounds like it starts with a *k*, so they put it in the club name. I know all this 'cause my big brother played right tackle on the high school football team that made the state finals. He got his goldstone heart for playing hurt and later graduating with grades good enough to qualify him for college."

"Who gave him the goldstone heart?" asked the chorus.

"Frank." Robert looked pleased with himself.

With one voice, the chorus parroted, "Frank gives hearts to football players?" We thought about that for a short minute, and I spoke up.

"Wrinkled ol' loner Frank gives out goldstone hearts to team-playing young men, and Frank gives our dancing parents goldstone hearts. I believe it 'cause you say it, but I don't understand, and I don't think we have solved the KKK question yet."

Everyone finished off their favorite pop with a drug-store-blues slurf on the straw.

"Let's some of us go over to Karen's Koffee Klatch café and see if we can overhear anything of value. Donnie, tell Janie what's happened here so you can listen at the Komfy Kozy Kave-inn for clues."

Melvin spoke up. "I'll report anything I hear at my uncle's Kolaches and Koffee Korner store."

Robert volunteered, "I'll keep my ears open around the Knuckles, Knees, and Koncussion club meetings."

I closed the meeting with, "We'll keep looking for meaningful clues to connect KKK, goldstone hearts, and Frank. Let's be grateful KKK is not that spooky KluKluxKlan in our small town."

Chapter Four

TEETER-TOTTER HANDCART

After school the next day, Robert shared some football gossip that added to our accumulation of clues. "You're not going to believe this! I had to hear it twice from two different football players before I could believe it myself!"

"What? What are you talking about?" came in unison from the chorus.

"Talk about dumb stunts! Some of the high school boys took the railroad teeter-totter handcart for a joy ride the evening before the big football game." Robert enjoyed the sensation this news was causing.

I responded to Melvin's elbow in my ribs by describing the cart the railroad work crew used to maintain the safety of the tracks. It was a platform of wood mounted on four railroad wheels, and there was an axle gear that would get the car rolling if the pump poking through the platform was pumped. The pump reminded us of a teeter-totter, so that's what we named it.

From the Meanderthaller chorus came a stutter of, "Who stole the handcart?"

"How many?"

"How did they get it out of the storage shed?"

"Isn't the shed locked?"

"Which way did they go—and why?"

Robert swallowed a spoonful of hot fudge sundae and continued, "All I know is it was some of the football team players. They just slid the storage shed doors open. I guess there was no padlock—I mean, why lock-up something nobody in their right mind would steal?"

Heads nodded in agreement.

"They wrestled the teeter-totter handcart out onto the main tracks and started pumping."

The chorus couldn't resist. "Which way did they go? Which way did they go?" We sounded like that cartoon character.

"They were smart enough to head south. North would have taken them too close to civilization: the drive-in theater, a couple of homes, and with the highway running parallel to the tracks, they risked being spotted. South meant open country: farm land and the Terrell Truck Stop where beer could be obtained."

The chorus yipped, "Beer! None of them are old enough to buy beer, and they shouldn't be drinking beer anyway."

Robert kept talking, "They got around the legal age limit by 'liberating' the beer."

The Meanderthallers sat silent as we contemplated the nerve of the flea-brains who would borrow the teeter-totter handcart, risk stealing—even if they called it 'liberating'—beer, and then brag about it.

"Me and the rest of the team got an earful of gossip after practice today. Everyone heard what great exercise it was to work the teeter-totter that far. Whoever they were, they went as far as the truck stop, shagged a case of beer, and ran back to the handcart without being caught. It must have been almost dark when they got back to town, which meant they had chugged that case of beer by the time they crossed the trestle."

We looked at each other, but we just knew Frank wouldn't have been on the trestle. Doc Bucky had a medical word, but Frank called it bad night-sight. Frank just didn't get out after it got dark—usually.

Robert continued, "Anyways, they ended their evening by tipping the handcart over in front of the depot just for kicks. I imagine they were too full of beer to maneuver it back into the shed. The policeman found the cart when he made his rounds. He drove over to Mr. Eady's house and made him wake up the track work crew to put the cart back in the shed."

My mouth was open before my brain got in gear. "It wouldn't take a genius to figure out who pulled the stunt, but our policeman has problems. He wouldn't want to cause a fuss with some of the town leaders when they found out what their sons did."

"Take a breath, Mary Clare. Let me finish," Robert went on, "Mr. Eady had a big, old padlock put on the shed door. No more midnight rides for whoever."

"Whomever," Kay jumped on the proper English before I could respond, which is just as well. It's a safe bet those flea-brains are the sons of some of the town's leading citizens, like the town councilmen. Those men decide the cop's salary and vote on special favors like a new cop car with a siren and overhead flash-bar lights.

The Meanderthallers sat and sipped and strained to make a connection between the stolen/borrowed handcart, the beer-run by flea-brains, Frank and the trestle. Reckafrex! Clues, clues, and more clues leading everywhere but to the clean, clear truth. We scattered like chickens when my dad came in the front door to use the pay phone again.

Later, I was sitting alone in the back booth when I overheard one of the dads, "Good job, son. That was well done. A quick, clean job, and I must say, you surprised me. Good job." His voice carried across the whole store.

But—his son doesn't have a job. The son receiving the compliment was one of the flea-brains we suspect of borrowing the teeter-totter handcart, and we know the dad paying the compliment hated the ground Frank walked on. My curiosity brain cells went on high alert, and I started talking to myself. I do that a lot 'cause nobody likes to sit and listen when my imagination starts rolling. So! The dad hated Frank. Frank is dead. The son gets a compliment for a job well done. Is there a connection?

I interrupted myself to finish my Green Mountain. Let's see, where was I? Why would anybody bother to hate Frank? The people in town acted like Frank was invisible. They didn't bother him; they ignored him. I bet they don't even know he's dead. Would they care if they knew he was dead? How would they react?

"Mary Clare, your face will freeze if you think that hard too long." Kay, the preacher's daughter, was walking by with her mother.

"Hello, Kay and Mrs. Priester. I was trying to remember something Frank said. Kay, were you with the Meanderthallers the day Frank was looking at the spire of the Catholic Church sticking way up almost cloud high?"

"I don't know. What did he say about the church?"

"Frank said, 'That spire is going to slice into that cloud. It reminds me of seeing the spires of the Kremlin hiding in a cloud.' Then he kinda coughed and made like he couldn't talk until his throat cleared. He quick changed the subject, but I remembered that remark, and next trip to the library, I looked up the Kremlin church."

Mrs. Priester laughed, "Mary Clare, the Kremlin is a very famous old church in the middle of Moscow, Russia."

"I know. I looked it up when I went to the library. I didn't see a church; I saw an awful grey building in Moscow, Russia. Was it a church? On TV, I've seen a gaggle of sad and angry-looking old men in black coats clustered on the balcony of the Kremlin to watch a military parade."

Kay asked the $64,000.00 question: "How would Frank know what the Kremlin looks like? What would Frank be doing in Russia? It's an awful long way from there to here."

Kay and I were off and running, dribbling questions back and forth with Mrs. Priester listening open-mouthed. "Is the Kremlin somehow connected to Frank living here in this small-town-America?"

"Was he hiding out here because of something that happened there?"

"Come to think of such a thing, this would be an ideal 'no where' to disappear into."

Russia! Kremlin! Communists!"

"James Bond!"

"Murder! Spies! Espionage—or however you say that word."

"Okay, girls, enough unanswerable questions. What imaginations! You should write a book when this is over, but now I have shopping to finish. You girls can continue this another time," and away they went.

I returned to talking to myself. Eeeecats and little doglets! I don't even want to put Frank in the same sentence with communism. Some of the grown-ups here have such an attitude about communism and communists that they could think Frank's death would be good riddance of a communist, but what if Frank wasn't a communist? Then his death would really be a murder for no good reason. Or a murder for a reason we don't know yet.

Wait a minute! The dictionary defines murder as a death due to premeditation—I had to look up premeditation: a killing on purpose, a thought-out plan to kill. What could ever make a murder a murder for a good reason? Lemme think! There is an old saying—oh! Yeah! "The only good communist is a dead communist." Good or bad communist, there is no reason for someone to murder our friend Frank. First, there would have to be a trial and lawyers and a jury and witnesses and… and…and…but it's too late to do Frank any good.

Crickety! The true identity of KKK, the possibility of communists, and what else is going on in this little town that we Meanderthallers don't know yet. Maybe another Green Mountain will cool my overheated brain cells.

Chapter Five

GOONS and PINKERTONS

Everybody in town heard the sirens, and then, the silence. By the sound, we Meanderthallers knew it hadn't been the fire siren, so it must have been the cop car and maybe the sheriff. We bailed out of the booth, grabbing for jackets, and trying not to run, but we had to go see.

"Children! Children!"

We screeched to a halt as one of the town D.O.L.L.'s tottered away from the drug store counter and waved her hands like she was shooing chickens.

"Children, quickly go to the back of the store. You will be safe in the store room."

It took every muscle in us to stop race walking, smile, and retreat to the back booth out of sight of the D.O.L.L.—that's our abbreviation for Dear Old Lavender-haired Lady. Safe wasn't what we had in mind, but ignoring the D.O.L.L. was not an option. So back to the back booth we retreated!

"Who's got my jacket? This one's my color, but it's too small for me." Nancy tried to wriggle out of a pink plaid jacket. "Little C, this must be your jacket. I grabbed it by mistake."

EJ and Robert traded denim bomber jackets, and I just waited until my green jacket with the knit collar got dumped on the table. We kept sneaking a peek over the top of the booth, hoping the coast would clear and we could get out the front door and go see about the sirens. We sat and stewed, peeking and waiting and watching. We didn't have to wait long. The answer came race walking through the front door, heading straight for the back booth—Donnie! He arrived short of breath but long on answers.

"Did you hear 'em? I'm so out of breath I can't talk. Gimme a slurp of that root beer, and I'll tell you what happened."

While Donnie caught his breath, I did a quick whisper to Melvin who had that 'huh?' look again. "Donnie's family owns and runs that big ol' barn of a place called the Komfy Kozy Kave-inn just off Main Street."

"Oh! Thanks, Mary Clare. It looks like a hotel, but I see old people coming 'n going 'n sitting on the porch like they live there."

"Pretty sharp, Melvin. The first floor is hotel rooms for short-stay tourists and traveling folks. The second floor is for old folks who can still climb stairs. It is a pretty basic boarding house."

"Boarding house? Does that mean they get meals with their rooms?"

"Right again. Donnie's Ma does the cooking and cleaning. His Pa keeps the place from fallin' apart. The oldest daughter JoAnn does the bookkeeping. The family has a place to eat 'n sleep; the kids carry out the trash and do chores. The family lives on the third floor."

Donnie put the root beer down, and away he went about the sirens. "Okay! Okay! Here's the scoop. First, I gotta' remind you, Frank lived on the second floor. He chose the corner room by the fire escape. Frank always paid in cash for room and board on the first day of the month. He paid extra cash to have Ma do his shirts and pants."

The chorus jumped in with, "Okay! Okay! Frank was a neatnik! We got the picture. Now, what about the sirens?"

"Ma says she's never seen clothes so easy to wash and iron. She didn't recognize the brand names and wasn't about to risk the money by asking questions, but she loved to gossip. It bugged her that nobody cared about fine clothing, particularly when the clothing belonged to a dark-skinned old man."

Donnie paused for a root beer slurp, and the chorus begged him, "Enough with the portrait. Explain the sirens. P-u-l-e-e-zzz!"

"Okay! Okay! A big, black car drove up to the Komfy Kozy Kave-inn, and three guys got out. They walked in like they had a plan. One guy stayed in the car and kept the motor running. The three walked in, went right up to the check-in desk where my Pa was sittin' and smokin'."

"This is better than radio. Then what happened?" Nancy, our actress-in-training, was on the edge of her seat.

"The lead stranger asked what room was Frank's, and he wanted a key. When Pa asked who they were and why they should have a key, the lead guy drew a cannon of a pistol and stuck it in Pa's face. Pa just reached up and handed 'em the spare key to Frank's room. The room number was right there on the tag. The three goons headed for the stairs to the second floor."

"Guns! Strangers in dark suits! I can just see this on TV!"

"Nancy, put a cork in it! Let Donnie tell the rest!" The chorus wanted more.

"Ma was in the first floor sun room, resting a minute, and when she saw and heard what she saw and heard, she reached over for the pay phone, dropped a dime, and dialed the police office and then the sheriff to report a hold-up happening."

I piped up in admiration: "Cool catnip! That's quick thinking, and I bet those calls got fast response!"

"You heard the cop car whoop'n and a wail'n. Trouble was, the strangers could hear him coming too. They bailed out the fire escape door—"

"OH NOOOOO!" from the Meanderthaller chorus.

"Yep! Pa had just painted the landing. Those goons hit that wet paint and skidded off the landing and through the wooden guard rail on the second floor. They crash landed on the firewood pile just as the cop pulled up out front with the sheriff eating his muffler. I mean, we almost had a two-car accordion." Donnie stopped to guzzle on a root beer somebody handed him.

"Then what happened? How many of those goons did the sheriff catch?" came in unison from the Meanderthaller chorus.

"The driver of the big black car heard the sirens coming, so he backed away and eased around the corner of the Komfy Kozy Kave-inn just as the three goons came crashing down on the wood pile. Somehow, they dragged each other to the car, and by the time Ma, Pa, the cop, and the sheriff quit shouting at each other, the goons were long gone."

"Oh No! Gone? Splitsville?" from the chorus.

"Yeah! 'Cept JoAnn got the license number. There is a state wide all-points bulletin for a black car with four guys in dark suits. The CB network is hummin'. Three of the rats have big pistols in shoulder holsters." Donnie reached for his sister's root beer.

"They need to alert the hospitals and doctors' offices. A fall from the second floor onto a pile of wood might have done more than bruise some back-sides!" I snickered at my own cleverness.

Donnie swallowed and started talking again, "Well they are short one of those big pistols."

"What?"

"How do you know?"

"More!"

"Tell us more!"

"One of those goons dropped his pistol trying to limp to the car and drag his buddy at the same time. I found it between the wood pile and the tire tracks left when that big black car kicked gravel gettin' out of there."

"DONNIE! Don't tell me you touched that gun after all those lectures about gun safety!" I was making like a parrot 'cause that's the line we hear in school all the time. Most of us have handled guns since we were littler kids. Donnie knows enough about guns not to shoot somebody or himself but—

"Okay! Okay! Calm down. I tried to report the gun-on-the-ground, but the grown-ups were too busy yelling at each other, so I picked it up and stuck it under the back stairwell. You know that area the dogs have dug out so they can get in out of the weather."

"Your dogs like that dug out area better than the fancy dog house Frank built for them." EJ slipped that in without breaking Donnie's concentration.

"That big ol' gun is wedged in solid. It is safe there until we figure out what to do next!" Donnie polished off a root beer and tried to look serious.

"Donnie, you really did the right thing. NOW hear this!" I tried to sound like Doc Bucky does when he uses his WWII Naval Commander voice. "Now hear this! Nobody but nobody touches that gun for no reason, good or bad reason! No good or bad reason." I stopped to see if everyone got the message even if I massacred the delivery.

"Remember last year when Jimmy blew a hole through the roof of the Coast to Coast Store? Some total idiot had slipped a live round in one of the display guns, and when Jimmy was shopping for a new rifle, Ted Fred, the owner, told him to 'Go ahead, squeeze the trigger.' Jimmy did not slide the bolt back to check 'n see that the gun was truly not loaded. He just squeezed the trigger like Ted said to do—KaBlammmm!" Every eye of the Meanderthallers was focused on me, and they were truly listening, so I again ordered. "No excuses. No reasons. Nobody touches that gun until we figure who we can tell and not get yelled at."

A slow deep breath later, I added, "We need to find out who those goons were and what Frank had that they wanted. From what Donnie says, those goons were exactly where they wanted to be but got interrupted before they could complete their mission successfully—er—successfully complete their mission."

We agreed Frank was worth the trouble it was taking to uncover the truth, but what could Frank have that four goons would make a special trip to get.

"And how did they know Frank was dead?" Melvin hit us right between the eyes. "Frank was your friend, but you didn't know him very well, did you? You just accepted him and felt lucky to have a grown-up for a friend."

One word came out. "Ouch!" 'cause the truth hurt. One strange old man had been an unexpected gift to our lives, and we just never asked who or why, and now it was too late. We Meanderthallers headed home for supper with a lot on our minds. Who? Why? What? So many clues, so cloudy the picture. The more we learn, the less we know.

We were in school so we didn't get to see it, but we sure heard about it. It? It was the sight of the local railroad repair crew working the teeter-totter so fast, the handcart almost left the rails. Seems Mr. Raditch, the depot agent, got a totally unofficial, heads up message over the telegraph from his friend, the agent in Fort Dodge. The tracks had been cleared so the Pinkerton Detective Agency men would be the only train on the rails. They had company orders to make the run up so they could check the "NO TRESPASSING" signs on the trestle.

Melvin had that blank look on his face again.

"Metal posts support metal 'NO TRESPASSING' signs at the approaches to the trestle. We kids used to obey the signs and skid down the gravel grade to No Name Creek until Jerome slipped on the hop scotch bridge we built out of big rocks. He broke his arm."

Melvin made a face and hugged his arms like he was protecting himself.

Anyways, from then on, we were told to use the trestle to cross the creek. We were real careful to be sure the train wasn't coming when we were on the trestle, but that teeter-totter handcart was awful quiet once it got going, and suddenly we'd hear, "Hey you kids! Can't you read?"

Yikes! Mr. Eady and the work crew had caught us. Quick, we'd think of some excuse like, "The local hunters have been using the signs to sight in their hunting rifle scopes, and the bullet splats covered up the words 'NO TRESPASSING.'"

Usually, Mr. Eady and the crew would nod their heads, start pumping the teeter-totter to get going again, and we would hear them promising not to forget to remember to remind each other to tell Mr. Raditch to order new signs.

Anyways, when Mr. Raditch, Floyd, read the Morse code saying the Pinkertons were on their way, he went tearing out of the depot yelling, "Pinkertons coming! Pinkertons coming to investigate the signs by the trestle. Ben Eady, get your men ready and get moving. Put these new signs up double quick."

He kept yelling until the guys lollygagging around the work room heard him. They had to find Ben Eady to unlock the padlock so they could get to the teeter-totter handcart. Ben Eady had the only key. They found Ben in the middle of a chocolate donut and cup of coffee at Karen's Koffee Klatch Cafe. He shoved the rest of the donut in, gulped the last of the coffee, and ran all the way to the shed. He fumbled in his overall pockets, and then realized the key was in the jacket he left hanging on the booth hook of the Koffee Klatch.

Floyd kept yelling, "Pinkertons are coming! Get to gettin'! Move! Move!"

To save Ben Eady from a heart-attack run to the café, and then back to the shed, the guys used a big screw driver to lever the latch off one side of the doors. The padlock stayed locked; the whole door swung open and pulled out the hinges. Anyways, they rolled the handcart out and started teeter-tottering, only to stop and reverse as Floyd came running out of the depot luggage room yelling, "Stop! Stop! Wait for the new signs!"

That is the only time anyone ever heard the brakes squeal on the handcart as the work crew tried to get the thing stopped. Floyd handed over the brand new signs and a tool kit and started yelling, "Go! Go! Get those signs up before the Pinkertons get here!"

That's when the work crew, under the leadership of Ben Eady, made that teeter-totter handcart fly.

Some of the hunter types at the Koffee Klatch were yappin' about putting some dings in the new signs just to ruffle the feathers of the Pinkertons, but the policeman persuaded them to wait. "The Milwaukee Railroad company hires the Pinkerton Detective Agency to protect their assets, and the sooner those Pinkerton's see the signs telling people to stay off the trestle, the sooner the Pinkerton's will leave. It don't make no never mind to the railroad as long as Frank's ever being on the trestle was in clear violation of 'NO TRESPASSING' signs. Those signs will put the company in the legal clear."

The arrival of the Pinkertons in a sure 'nuff four-door sedan car specially equipped with railroad wheels drew a crowd, including us Meanderthallers just out of school. We stood in front where we could see the strange men in fancy, three-piece suits and funny stiff brimmed hats open the door of a regular car and step out onto the depot platform. They visited with Mr. Raditch, and he made the ride with them to the trestle. As soon as the Pinkertons went out and saw the signs, they returned to leave Mr. Raditch on the depot platform.

EJ came up with the question of the day. "Does that car have a real train horn? Can you just see some old farmer getting close to the railroad crossing, and hearing a train horn just as a car crosses ON the railroad tracks?"

We Meanderthallers almost fell on the depot platform laughing at the thought.

"I wonder how many pickup trucks they put in the ditch with that horn."

That did it! We slapped each other on the back and got to laughing so hard, the cop had to threaten to tell our folks we were being nuisances. We quieted down to giggling.

Then we watched as Mr. Eady and the repair crew teeter-tottered away from the station. They were headed toward the trestle to put the dinged-up signs back and retrieve the brand new signs. We heard Mr. Raditch mutter to himself as he went back in the depot to telegraph a "thanks" and give his friend in Fort Dodge the details.

"No sense in using new signs just to provide fresh targets for the local hunter types and their rifle scopes."

Chapter Six

FUNERAL? FUNERAL!

Funeral? Jiminy Cricket! We had been so busy listening to gossip and trying to figure what really happened to Frank, we hadn't thought about a funeral. Funerals cost money, and we started worrying Frank might end up in the county poor folk's part of the cemetery. That would mean no real grave, no real casket, and no permanent marker. It would be hard for us to visit him, and in no time, we could forget this old man who took time to be our friend. We had no idea how much a funeral would cost, but we were determined Frank would have a casket, a proper send-off, and a grave with a marker. We started digging in our jeans and planning to raid our piggy banks when Janie found us meeting in the back booth. She came skidding up to the booth and announced, "Money! Frank had money!"

"Shhhhhhhhh!" hissed out of the chorus, and we sneak-peeked over the back of the booth to check for eavesdroppers. "What money?"

"Where?"

"How much?"

"Wilma Jo was helping Ma clear Frank's stuff out of his room at the Komfy Kozy Kave-inn. It was just stuff you'd expect in an old man's room like clothes and shoes and stuff—and rocks. Ma and Wilma Jo were gonna throw the rocks away, but I said save them for Mary Clare. They're in an old paint bucket for you to pick up whenever."

"Money! You said there was money, Janie. What money? Where's the money?" hissed from the chorus.

"There wasn't anything suspicious until they got to an old Army-type foot locker. You know, like in the movies. A plain, dark-green, big ol' metal box with latch locks. It wasn't locked, so they opened it up, and—" she paused for a long drag on EJ's root beer float.

"What?"

"What was in the foot locker?"

"C'mon, Janie! Spill the beans!" from the Meanderthaller chorus.

Janie barely whispered, "Books."

"Books? What kind of books? Where's the money?"

"Books lined up on trays. Neat trays full of book on lots of subjects! They didn't dig any further than the top tray full of music books, music tablets, and music folders. They were about to close the foot locker when Wilma Jo saw the corner of a bill. She opened a music book and there were hundred-dollar bills inside."

We Meanderthallers sat in shocked silence. I guess each of us was thinking how we would have handled finding money, much less hundred-dollar bills. It really slapped us to think of having to choose: honesty or grab and run. Wow! Just the thought of one single hundred-dollar bill strains a person's honesty nerve.

Janie polished off J.R.'s root beer float and started talking again, "Ma screamed and Pa came clattering up the stairs with his baseball bat on the ready! He thought the goons were back. When he saw the money, he dropped the bat and almost had a heart attack. The three of them put the hundred-dollar bills back in the music book, closed up the foot locker, latched all the latches, and went to call the cop—er—policeman and the sheriff."

I piped up "Called both law men? I guess it means double the honesty if two people are involved, huh?"

Janie agreed. "Guess they thought two law men would think of all the questions and keep each other honest. The sheriff is gonna take the foot locker and try to lift some finger prints off stuff. He is also going to check to be sure it's real money, not counterfeit. Our policeman sputtered, but he agreed the sheriff had more time and better equipment, so together they lugged that heavy foot locker down to the sheriff's car. I'm going back to the Kave-inn to see what's developing. See you later, alligators."

We were sitting and thinking when Mr. Murrey delivered a fresh root beer float for EJ. Seems Janie paid for one on her way out, and Mr. Murrey took a wild guess it was for one of the Meanderthallers.

"Well, it would seem there will be no problem paying for Frank's funeral." This $64,000 observation came from EJ. "But how do you plan a funeral? We've all attended funerals, but all we had to do was dress up, sit still, and listen 'cause somebody already arranged for the place, the music, and someone to say a few words."

The Meanderthallers froze as they saw the signal of my radar ears at work. Everyone knew I couldn't see very good, but I had ears that would rival a cat. When I hear something nobody else hears, I close my eyes and start aiming my head until my ears center on the target. Everybody started looking to see what had broken through the clatter of our chatter.

Little C saw what I heard. "It's Mr. LaFloy talking to "Jim." Just a minute and I'll ask them to join us!" She slid under the booth table and was up the aisle before any of us could try to stop her.

"Jim? Jim who?" Melvin was new in town and didn't know about my mother.

"Jim is my mom." I smiled at Melvin's look. "When she was 13, she became the piano player in her dad's orchestra. He nicknamed her 'Jim' after a comic strip character who was always half-a-step behind, not too quick, and mostly late. Now she is a wife, a mother, a talented musician, and one cool person." The Meanderthallers nodded. "She is pretty famous 'cause she can play any tune in any key just hearing the music, or she reads it off little Tune-dex cards. She claims to 'play by soul.'" I stopped 'cause Little C returned to the booth with Jim and Mr. LaFloy, and a tray of Coke Floats. Next thing we knew, we had fresh Coke Floats in front of us and two grown-ups listening as we described our dilemma.

"Frank didn't have family to arrange a funeral."

"We are Frank's friends which makes us unofficial family."

"And we want him to have a funeral with casket, funeral service, a ride in the hearse."

"And a grave out at the cemetery."

"An' a fancy headstone!"

The Meanderthallers didn't give Mr.LaFloy or my mother a chance to answer.

"And Frank had enough money to pay for everything."

"We need your help setting up a right proper, official, first-class funeral."

"Will you please help us?"

Mr. LaFloy looked at Jim and handed her a handkerchief out of the breast pocket of his suit jacket. She dabbed at the tears and gave each of us a hug-smile. (If you don't understand, I feel sorry for you. Some people can hug without grabbing you, and it is a good thing for touchy people who don't like to be touched—like me). Anyways, she volunteered to play for the viewing and the service. Mr. LaFloy said he would set up with the Lightly Funeral Home to have a closed-casket viewing on the evening before the funeral service.

No one had ever seen Frank in any of the three churches in town, so we figured none of the ministers or priest would volunteer to say a few words. That's when we found out more about Mr. LaFloy. We all knew he had been one of the first Marines sent into Korea, and was wounded right off which landed him in a hospital for a couple years before he got to come home. What none of us knew was that he was a Marine Chaplain, and he volunteered to say a few words. In fact, he seemed glad for the opportunity. Mr.LaFloy offered to coordinate with Lightly Funeral Home and polish off the details of a casket, a cemetery plot, a hearse ride, and any other funeral arrangement details.

Wow! Just like that we had the problem of a proper funeral for our friend solved. The meeting of the Meanderthallers broke up. Little C and I walked home with our mother who was going on about how proud she was of us for caring about a funeral for Frank.

"I'll play some of his favorite tunes during the Wednesday evening viewing."

My jaw dropped. "Favorite tunes? How do you know what tunes Frank liked?"

"It was at one of the dances in the Central Ballroom on West Lake Okoboji last summer. Your father noticed Frank standing out on the veranda listening. Your father went out to invite Frank to come in, but Frank seemed anxious about being in the light. Your Father took a chair out so Frank could be comfortable and asked what tunes Frank liked. I played "Stardust," "Deep Purple," and other easy-listening tunes. Frank seemed to prefer the minor key music like "Dark Eyes." When the dance was over, Frank had disappeared, or we would have given him a ride back to town. From that incident on, we would occasionally see Frank in the shadows, and I would play "Dark Eyes" for him. At his funeral, I will play the tune he wrote and gave me."

I squeaked, "Frank gave you a tune he wrote? When?" Little C was just as dumb-founded as I was. She stood there stuttering.

Mother laughed at our shocked expressions. "Frank must have been a talented musician somewhere, but he lived in quiet shadows here. When did he give me that tune? I remember being at home alone, you kids were playing baseball on the Tax Payers League field, and your Father was uptown, when the doorbell rang. There was Frank. He would not come in and seemed very nervous. He handed me a folder with hand-written music and gently squeezed my hand.

"From one musician soul to another," was all he said before he slipped away.

"It is a beautiful, haunting melody he titled "Gypsy Jewels." I will work it in during his funeral, but I will not say anything. It will be a gift to one musician soul from another."

We three girls walked the three blocks home quietly racing our thoughts to the funeral for a friend.

The County Coroner returned from his Minnesota Muskie fishing vacation and released Frank's body for burial. Mr. LaFloy told Lightly Funeral Home to put out the word that a closed-casket viewing would occur Wednesday evening. A funeral Service was to be held from their parlor Thursday morning at 10:00 followed by a motorcade procession to the town cemetery. By that time everybody in town knew there was enough money found in Frank's books to pay for a casket, a plot at the cemetery and the hearse ride out there.

Everybody came to the closed-casket viewing just to see who else would show up. We Meanderthallers were strategically sprinkled all around the place intending to overhear any gossip. Our hope was that someone would slip and say something that would give us a clue, a lead to the truth of Frank's death. I looked up to catch a signal. Mr. LaFloy gave me the hand signal for Stop! Stay! Which I did. He walked right up to me with a smile on his face that was supposed to put me at ease. Before he could say anything the whole gang of Meanderthallers surrounded us.

"Relax, kids. I'm here to tell you Meanderthallers that you don't have to go to school tomorrow. You need to be at Frank's funeral service, and you all can ride out to the cemetery with me or Doc Bucky."

We almost gave a cheer at the thought of no school, but then it hit us: We would be going to a sure 'nuff funeral for a sure 'nuff friend. Death had never been this personal before. We had been to funerals for family, but this was about a friend; someone who liked us just because. It really was a different feeling.

Thursday morning the Lightly Funeral Home parlor was packed, and people were standing in the extra room with more people piled in the hall. Someone on the staff turned up the P.A. system volume to the max. I am glad 'cause Marine Chaplain Mr. LaFloy really let the town have it. It was not the garden variety "few words at a funeral." I'm glad I had my note-taking-tablet; as best I can remember, this is pretty close to what he said.

"No one here knew this man. No one in this town took the time to know who he was, what he was, if he had family, or if he felt good, bad, or indifferent that day. Would it have made a difference to you to know he had money? What if—? What if he had been an artist? An engineer? An architect? What if he was one of those people put into witness protection? What if he was given a new identity? For what reason? What if he was a national hero? What if he had a family he was protecting by disappearing to this small town? We were content that he minded his own business. What was his business? Did any of us ever ask, 'How's business?' Was it easier to not ask—or care?

"Our young people were his contact with humanity. They didn't care that his skin was dark. I remember when one of them gave Frank a bar of her Grandmother's lye soap telling Frank it would really get his skin clean. Another one of our young people said his Mother's warning about too much sun causing permanent skin damage had real meaning after seeing Frank's permanent tan. You laugh? How many of us saw skin permanently darker than our 'white' skin and branded him a man-of-color? Was it easier to hate than consider that people of the Mediterranean or Baltic countries are commonly darker-skinned than us 'white' folk? And so what if he had a few cells of another race that left his skin dark? I ask 'so what' even while I recognize that there are those among this gathering who treat even the hint of color as a crime, a difference worthy of terrible punishment. Was Frank's death truly an accident or the result of arbitrary judgment and execution for a matter of skin color?

"Doc Bucky asked that I be one of the observers at the autopsy. Frank's body bore the scars of beatings. His feet were bent and painful to see. Yet, he walked, appreciating the freedom to come and go without restriction. There was a tattoo on his forearm. The tattoo suggests he had been imprisoned. Where? Why? By whom? The answers to these questions are sought in an effort to give this old man identity. Pictures and a description of the tattoo have been air-mailed to Washington D.C. in an attempt to find this man's place in time.

"His death has been listed as accidental. Our young people must wonder at the grown-ups who so cavalierly dismiss a death. As a community, we missed the opportunity to discover the history of this stranger in our midst. When we put his body in the ground, will the memory fade and disappear so easily? Out of sight and out of mind? Praise to our young people who gave this old man, this fellow human being, dignity, a sense of worth, and the joy of knowing someone cared. Too soon some of us have gotten old, set in our ways, threatened by someone 'different,' defensive about tradition, and too late we realize we missed a chance to be 'schmart.'"

Mr. LaFloy ended with a short prayer thanking God for volunteering to be God and deciding where Frank would spend eternity. My mother played and everybody sang "Amazing Grace." I think Frank would have approved.

The crowd was awful quiet as they headed for their cars. We Meanderthallers felt like crying and cheering; we were humbled and proud all at the same time. We all went up and shook Mr. LaFloy's hand. He gave us separate hugs, and he gave Little C a real Marine salute when she lisped, "Themper Fi." We headed for Doc Bucky's big Buick and Mr. LaFloy's old bomb of a souped up Mercury. It was creepy to be the two cars immediately behind the hearse as the procession headed for the cemetery. In a few years, we might realize what that meant, but living the moment was straight excitement.

Accidentally or on purpose, the grave site chosen for Frank had a perfect line-of-site at the trestle a mile northwest of the cemetery. Mr. LaFloy said a few more words as Frank's casket was lowered, and we Meanderthallers got to put a shovel full of dirt into the grave. It was spooky to hear the clumps of frozen dirt hit the casket. I was glad when everybody started scattering to their cars. Much more of this and I might'a started crying.

Chapter Seven

CLUES and MORE CLUES

It was a bright, sun-glare-off-the-snow day for Frank's funeral and grave-side service. Mom and I decided to walk home from the cemetery. She isn't all that tall, but Mom loves to walk, and she can keep up with anybody when she shifts into her overdrive walking gear. To avoid any offers of a car ride, I directed her to the cemetery back gate, and we slipped away from the crowd. We could cut across a pasture and intercept the blacktop road to town. I was just drawing breath to start telling the Frank story when she stopped. Flat out, both feet planted, STOP! She was looking down at the remains of a b-i-g bonfire.

Ol' smart mouth me blurted out, "That must have been some marshmallow-wienie roast party!"

Mom kinda shuddered and took a step, then another.

"Mom! What did I say?"

She stopped, turned, looked at me, and barely whispered, "Your father and I saw the cross burning as we drove home late Saturday night."

"Cross! Who would burn a—oh! My gosh! THAT KKK is for real? In our small town?"

"Yes, our little town has the largest cell of the KKK in the state."

My mind was going in all directions at the implications of those ashes. "But that means the dads of some of my friends have a dark side!"

The expression on my Mom's face was sad, and I couldn't identify exactly what other emotion her face was showing; it was like a shadow when a cloud blocks the sun shine. She whispered, "A very dark side."

Mom took my arm, and we walked away from the pile of ashes. She pointed west, and I looked where she was pointing. A train was starting to cross the trestle, and I remembered about Frank. When we came to the farmer's makeshift bridge over No Name Creek, I found a sunny place where we could sit and talk.

I pulled out my note-taking-tablet and started talking. Mom listened. She really focused and listened as I told about my first meeting Frank, his goldstone watch fob, his friendship, finding the body, the missing gloves and cap, the beer run handcart escapade, the dad who told his son "job well done," the goons, and the pistol. I finished by showing her the half a goldstone heart I had retrieved from the creek, as Frank's body was skidded up the No Name Creek bank.

"Mary Clare! You really have a way with words. Everything you and the Meanderthallers have collected needs to be documented. Every piece is important to the whole picture. It is every bit like putting a puzzle together. Keep digging. Keep listening. Tell the Meanderthallers I say 'Well done.' Ask for a volunteer or appoint someone to write down each clue. Some little piece of information gets forgotten if you don't write it down right away. When you look at it in a week or so, some other little piece will click, and the puzzle begins to make a picture."

I let out a deep sigh. Guess I had been holding my breath. "Thanks, it's been quite a load to carry. We just didn't know who to trust. We have tried to get our policeman interested. It is hard to find a grown-up who won't blow us off or make fun of us. The Meanderthallers voted to trust you. I promised them you would listen and help us—like you did with Frank's funeral arrangements."

Mom patted my shoulder before getting down to brass tacks. "Let's get that pistol in the hands of the sheriff. It is dangerous for it to be where just anyone could acquire it. You Meanderthallers are all familiar with guns, and you have done well but—temptation is a mighty power; let's remove the cause of a potential tragedy. Also, if the sheriff can trace the serial numbers, it might provide a clue to the identity of the goons."

We climbed to our feet, brushed the snow off our behinds, and started for home again. That's when I thought of Frank's hideout. Crickety! I didn't know if Frank knew I knew about that little cabin 'cause we never talked about it. Privacy was such a sacred concept that I had never even thought about peeking inside—not even through a window. Now what to do? I had loaded enough on mom for one sharing. I decided to hold off and let the discovery and recovery of the pistol blow over first and then tell her about the cabin. It had been a hidden hideout this long. A little longer wouldn't matter.

My mother told the sheriff about the goon-pistol first and then our local policeman. They both stopped whatever they were doing and ordered—well, the sheriff asked politely if we Meanderthallers would meet him in back of the Komfy Kozy Kave-inn. The policeman was crude, rude, and not polite at all in his orders for us to "show up or he'd hunt us down." That attitude sure didn't earn any respect points from us. Anyways, we gathered for the recovery of the gun dropped by the goon and stashed by Donnie. The local policeman and the sheriff stood around while Donnie crawled under the stairwell to reach up where he'd wedged it. Those two big men couldn't see it even when they got on their knees and used their big flashlights. No way were they gonna' reach in, up, or around where some creepy critter might bite 'em. Donnie had mentioned he'd seen a rat earlier, and then he winked at us. Putting a scare in a couple of grown-ups was a way for him to improve his level of importance in this adventure.

Donnie backed out and extended the pistol, butt first, to the sheriff. The sheriff accepted it and loudly let go half an expletive—well, he almost swore.

"It's a .45 caliber pistol like General Patton wore in the Second World War, only this one doesn't have pearl handles. What the he— pardon me kids, what the hooey did Frank have that earned such heavy-duty firepower?" The sheriff was wearing white cotton gloves, and he was being very careful examining the pistol.

First thing he did was open the cylinder—that's the round thing that holds the bullets. Then he dropped the bullets from the cylinder into his gloved hand. That made the pistol officially unloaded. You can tell I study guns in gun magazines, and I know the correct terminology, but I can't crochet a stitch. Anyways, the local policeman reached out to take the pistol, but the sheriff growled.

"Hands off! I'm sending all this to a finger-print expert in Sioux City. That's why I'm wearing these cotton gloves. Close as I figure it, we're gonna get two sets of prints off this pistol: one set from Donnie, and any other prints will belong to the goon who dropped it. If the goon was ever in the military or in prison, there'll be a record of his prints. We'll track his prints down. At least we have a better chance to ID—that's identify him, kids. We'll ID the goon, and then we'll know exactly who we are looking for."

I had my mouth open and words flying before he had time to draw another breath, "And if we know who he was, maybe you can help us find out why they wanted in Frank's room."

"What was in Frank's room that they wanted bad enough to stick a gun in my pa's face?" Donnie was really mad, "There is something stinky about total strangers busting in here and knowing exactly where they wanted to go."

"Yeah! And how are they connected to Frank's death? We Meanderthallers are still convinced Frank did not slip and fall off the trestle. Maybe the goons pushed him! Or they might—"

The sheriff caught me mid breath and regained the floor, "Mary Clare, you have a great imagination, but we can only guess until we get these prints ID'd. Let me get this gun packed and on its way. I promise to let you Meanderthallers know when we get any results."

He reached into his pocket and drew out a cellophane envelope with a clear plastic card inside. "Donnie, would you please put your fingers directly on this card? If we send a sample of your fingerprints, it will make identification of one set of prints easier."

Donnie carefully left his grimy finger prints on the card, and we watched as the sheriff put the card in the cellophane envelope. With the pistol placed on the bed of cotton and the finger print envelope slipped inside the box, the sheriff sealed it all up with packing tape. That's when the cop offered to run it down to the post office. The sheriff looked up but didn't let go of the box.

"Thanks, but I haven't seen Miss Nellie, the post master, for a while. Mailing this box will give me a chance to give her a hug and catch up on news of her sick father."

For some reason our town policeman didn't seem happy. We thought he should be glad for this chance to get some goons and their guns out of circulation, off the streets, booked and boxed. Instead, he stomped away, got in the town police car, and burned rubber as he drove away.

The sheriff glanced at the disappearing car, looked at us and said, "It's ok, kids. He's taking a lot of heat over you kids, and your stubborn belief that Frank was murdered. The town officials don't much care to have Frank's death turn out to be murder. They are concerned about the bad publicity. It won't look good to be known as the town where a harmless, old man got murdered by unknown killers for unknown reasons. It could end up costing tourist dollars, if people are afraid to stop and shop here."

He stopped licking the address label long enough to look at each of us, "Whatever your digging turns up, you kids keep digging. The truth can be uncomfortable, but the truth, the whole truth, nothing but the truth is the best foundation. Bet on it!"

His words were still bouncing around our brains the next afternoon. We were on our way to Mr. LaFloy's basement apartment-rec room. He had asked us to come, play pool or whatever, and listen to a story. The invitation was unusual, but we all knew about that professional pool table and the rack of pool cues. We might have tried to dodge if we had known the story would be told by Ronnie B. Ronnie B may be number one on the football team, but he was a minus 3 with the Meanderthallers. He's never done anything to us; it's just that he is SO big. No way would we agree to be alone in a room with that scary, big hulk.

Carefully, we single-filed into the basement and parked on super-neat bar stools. We had to put our feet on the rails 'cause our legs weren't long enough to reach the floor. We sat up straight as Mr. LaFloy came down the steps from the house with Ronnie B shaking the stairs right behind him.

Without a blink, Ronnie B parked on the edge of the pool table. I thought I saw the pool table sag when he put his weight on the corner. Now that's as ridiculous as thinking the stairs shook, and I caught myself realizing I was not being fair. Ronnie B started talking before I could think through my prejudice about enormous, great big—and my mouth dropped open as words and sentences started pouring out of a well-spoken young man! Boy! Did I feel embarrassed! I quick grabbed my note-taking tablet.

"Do you kids remember those choice words Mr. LaFloy laid on this town over us not treating Mr. Frank like we would want to be treated? Mr. LaFloy's talk at Mr. Frank's funeral caught me up long side my head. His talk made me stop and think. To me, Mr. Frank was that strange old man who would hang around during football practice. When coach would yell at him to 'Get outta the way, ol' man. You'll get hurt!' It made me mad. That old man wasn't in the way, plus the rumors had him giving the year's best players a present: a goldstone heart. Him hanging around watching us practice meant I had a chance to show him I was the best at playing linebacker. Just thinking of wearing that heart made me practice harder and try to play smarter.

"I'll never forget the evening Mr. Frank was in the shadows under the bleachers as I came off the practice field. He spoke my name and asked if I minded him giving me a couple pointers on playing linebacker. I was so startled, I just mumbled something, and he proceeded to give me two excellent tips. He promised me I would knock the coach's hat in the creek if I would get good at going backwards. He told me to start walking backward, work up to a run and practice going up stairs backwards at a run. It sounded weird, but I gave it a try. Talk about a challenge! At first, I spent most of the time tripping over myself and bruising my backside. I stayed with it, and I finally quit falling over my own big feet. By game time, I could run backwards better than anybody else on the team. What he didn't tell me was the difference it made in my dancing. My girl friend says I didn't step on her feet even once at the sock hop last week.

"My big sister didn't need to soak her feet in ice after that sock hop. She wondered who gave you dance lessons." Nancy almost fell off her bar stool trying to do a twirl.

Ronnie B turned red, gulped, and kept talking, "Frank's other tip was to watch the quarterback's eyes and let my peripheral—er—side vision take care of the player running at me. Next game, I intercepted one pass and knocked down another one 'cause I saw where the quarterback 'looked' the pass. For the first time, my dad didn't get on my case with criticisms. He didn't compliment my play; he just didn't make me feel like a clumsy dumb jock this time. I don't know how you kids feel about your dad. If you're like me, we don't have a choice. The commandment says to 'honor your father.' Too bad it doesn't include loving or feeling loved. I've spent my whole life trying to have my dad show me he likes being my dad. Trying to earn my dad's respect, I do what he says even when I know deep inside it ain't always the right thing to do. Or the right attitude to have, like Mr. Frank. My dad gets purple thinking about 'that dark skinned old bum.' To me, Mr. Frank looks like he spent way too much time in the sun, but my dad has a real 'bend in the twig' about foreigners—about 'darkies'—and well, I guess his dad had a bad experience with 'people of color' and—well, that old saying: 'as the twig is bent, so grows the tree' bent my dad's brain permanently. It made it hard for me to see Mr. Frank as a good ol' guy trying to help when all my dad could see was an old bum with dark skin. What am I saying? Why did I ask Mr. LaFloy to referee—er—call this gathering?"

"Yeah, you big galoot! Get to the point."

"What are you saying that will help us find the truth to Frank's death?" The chorus was not happy.

"Okay! Here it is! You kids are looking for the truth about Mr. Frank's death. Well, maybe I was part of Mr. Frank's death."

We Meanderthallers started yelling and bailing off of our bar stools. The Marine part of Mr. LaFloy stood up and barked, "SIT DOWN! NOW!"

We sat down.

Ronnie B continued, "I think everybody in town knows some football players borrowed the railroad handcart for a joy ride after football practice. We were all real nervous about the Saturday game, and we thought a few beers would help us relax. As we teeter-tottered—yeah, everybody uses your term for working the handcart—as we teeter-tottered south of town I was sitting on the floorboard watchin' the scenery go by when we hit the curve past the Dust-Darner Crossing. I lost my balance and almost fell off the handcart.

"Woulda' served you right, you big dummy!" I slipped that in, but Ronnie B never paused.

"As I scrambled to get back on board, I thought I saw Mr. Frank hangin' on to the gate of that ol' gravel pit. I was so busy getting my balance and getting laughed at by the other guys, I didn't say anything. Then—kaboom! We almost hit a guy walkin' down the middle of the tracks. That guy was dressed all in camo clothes. He yelled at us as he jumped out of the way. None of us recognized him, but it kinda shook us up to come that close to runnin' over somebody. Boy! Could that weirdo yell! I won't repeat what he said, but I ain't never heard some of those words before. We all wondered who it was and what he was doin' spookin' down the middle of the railroad tracks. Camo clothes means hunting, but the middle of the tracks ain't the place to hunt, and it was getting' dark. I never said nothin' about maybe seeing Mr. Frank. I've heard he doesn't get out after dark 'cause of his eyes, and I doubted that it was Mr. Frank at all 'cause whoever it was had a holt onto that gate like he was hurtin' or out of breath. Whoever it was musta' heard the guy in camouflage yellin'.

"Anyways, we hit the Terrell Truck Stop and liberated—appropriated—okay! stole a case of Schlitz. We proceeded to chug that case of beer before we got back to town. I took my turn on the teeter-totter, but I was so loaded I don't remember the trip. I don't think we saw either the guy by the gate or the weirdo in camouflage; I don't even remember crossing the trestle. None of us had ever drunk that much beer before, and pumping that teeter-totter handcart made the beer circulate fast. We were blitzed, pie-eyed, out of it before we were half way back to town. When we reached the train station, we could hardly stand. No way could we put the handcart back in its shed, so we tipped it over off the track so it wouldn't be in the way of a freight train, and we staggered home to sleep off the beer.

Mr. LaFloy looked like he was going to say something, but Ronnie kept talking.

"Couple days later, my dad patted my shoulder and complimented me on a job well done. I asked him what he meant. He slapped me on the back and said the town was better off without a dark skinned bum cluttering up the place. It took me a full minute to figure out what he was talking about. My dad thought we kids had knocked Mr. Frank off the trestle. My dad just assumed we had done it and done it on purpose. For once, he was proud of me—for something I could never, ever do. Please! Please! Like I told Mr. LaFloy, I need you to understand. I DON'T KNOW! I don't remember, and that's the truth of it."

We sat in silence trying to think through what we had just heard. Mr. LaFloy thanked us for our courtesy in coming, listening and not judging Ronnie B until we had heard from the other three beer-guzzling, handcart borrowers. Immediately, Ronnie B gave up the names of the other three guys, and Mr. LaFloy promised to let us know the results of his interviews.

Little C stood up, walked over to Ronnie B and gave him a hug—well, hugged his leg. Her sensitive heart picked up there was a hurting, good little kid inside that great big body. That big hulk started crying like a baby. Next thing I knew, it was a Ronnie B and the Meanderthallers group hugging with Mr. LaFloy in the middle handing out Kleenexes.

MUNICIPAL
TOWN

Chapter Eight

JOHNNIE T

"Hustle! Hustle! State Highway Patrol car pulling up and parking in front of the town hall. C'mon gang!" Donnie skidded up to the back booth and had to duck as we Meanderthallers race-walked up the aisle and out the drug store door. A state highway patrol car is a Meanderthaller magnet. A State Mounty means business for our local law enforcement team—policeman, lawyer, judge-mayor. Anyways, before he got the car engine turned off and the door open, most of us were standing on the curb waiting to see what was being delivered.

"Look out! JUMP!" The State Mounty didn't ask questions. He hopped onto the hood of the state patrol car as our local policeman laid a ten foot streak of rubber getting the town's cop car stopped next to the patrolman. Our policeman bailed out of the cop car yelling, "What'cha caught? Where is the law-breaker? Who gets to go in my jail? What'd he do to earn the bunk in my fine facility?"

The Highway Patrolman slid off the hood of the Patrol car, slapped slushy mud off the seat of his uniform pants and stood up—and up—and up. Crickity! He was a TALL man, and he didn't look happy. He glanced at us, then at our policeman, then back at us. I got the feeling our being there saved our policeman from a straighten up-stand down-now hear this talkin' to. It was obvious the slushy mud had soaked into the seat of the highway patrolman's uniform. It didn't look good, and I'll bet it wasn't comfortable. The patrolman walked straight at our policeman who almost tripped getting out of the way as the patrolman opened the passenger door of his car and reached inside.

What came out of the patrol car didn't look like a bad guy. He looked like an escapee from a Halloween party. He had a fancy pair of cowboy boots with camouflage pants tucked into the stitched leather boot tops. The belt looked like genuine rattlesnake skin with the biggest trophy belt buckle ever seen here 'bouts. A camouflage-white blast jacket hid most of a heavy duty hand knit sweater. His gloved hands removed the twin to Frank's fur-lined cap with ear flaps when he saw us girls, but it was the gloves I zeroed in on. Those were Frank's gloves!

"Hey, mister! What are you doing with Frank's gloves?" My yell stopped the show and drew some interesting reactions.

The town policeman had rushed ahead to hold the town hall door open for the patrolman and—and—and whoever was wearing Frank's gloves. He yelled at us, "Get lost! This tramp is going to jail right here, right now, and he doesn't have to tell you kids nothin'—er—anything."

The patrolman was still standing by the patrol car with—with—whoever that was with Frank's gloves. The guy kept grinning at me, and he just didn't fit the picture of a bad guy. Bad guys should be ratty looking with long hair and needing a shave. This guy didn't need a shave 'n he wore his hair like my Dad's, and my sister, Gee, would say he's good looking.

The patrolman looked at us and said, "You must be the kids Frank called his friends. This here is Johnnie T, and he would appreciate the opportunity to meet with you kids. Please come back in about an hour. We'll talk. Could you all meet us in the Mayor's Office?"

A car door slammed, and we all turned to see the county sheriff. The patrolman gave him a thank-goodness-you're-here greeting. The sheriff thanked him for giving Johnnie T a ride, then grabbed Johnnie T and gave him a big hug! The three men walked past the town cop—er—policeman who was still holding the town hall door open. I'm sure the stunned look on the faces of us Meanderthallers matched the bucket-of-cold-water look on the policeman's face. This was turning into a social gathering, not a book 'em and bag 'em opportunity. We decided to wait that long hour in the back booth of the soda fountain. Nobody said a thing for two minutes, and then we all started talking at once.

"Who? Who was Johnnie T?"

"Why? Why did he rate a friendly ride in a state highway patrol car?"

"How? How did the county sheriff know him?"

"Where? Where did he get Frank's gloves?"

"And what all had just happened?"

For once, the Meanderthallers sat silent, except for the sips and slurps. Then we broke out in a rash of wild guesses, but our wildest guesses could not provide a true answer to one single question. We sipped and sat and watched the second hand on the soda fountain clock go round and round. That hour took two days, but eventually the little hand clicked to the next number and we started the walk toward the Town Hall.

It was a good thing we turned the corner and walked up to the front doors when we did. One of the town D.O.L.L.'s was trying to get into the Town Hall. The first set of doors into the Town Hall is downright unfriendly, and it takes two of us to grab hold and pull hard to let anyone in.

"Wait just a moment, ma'am. We'll open the door for you!"

"Oh, thank you, children. You're parents must be proud of you." The D.O.L.L. followed the rules to wipe her feet on the mud grid. Then she continued through the lighter, easier set of inner doors we held open for her. Voila! We were all in. There are doors all the way down the long hall, and the D.O.L.L. headed for the grown-up library.

We tromped past the kid's library, the ladies and gentlemen's rooms, and the policeman's office with a desk in front of the one-cell jail.

Elizabeth dodged past the desk to peek around the corner to see if anyone was in the jail cell. "Empty!" She caught up with us just as we reached the mayor's office, which is right across from the Town Hall hall and big kitchen.

"In here, kids." came from the Town Hall hall. The patrolman and sheriff were seated across from the mayor at one of those long tables usually folded up and stashed in the closet. Johnnie T, with a bottle of Coca-Cola in his left hand, was sitting right next to the mayor.

"Help yourselves, and put a napkin under your pop bottle. We can't have rings marking up the table." continued the mayor as he pointed to a cooler full of bottles of pop. There was an opener on the side of the cooler, and you could hear that distinct *sprifff* as the bottle opened. Thank goodness not a one sprayed the area!

"Park yourself and get a couple cookies."

The local policeman came out of the hall kitchen balancing a big tray of cookies. The mayor helped himself and slid the tray down the table toward us. The policeman retreated to a chair in the corner where he could listen and see without being obvious.

He must realize he does not have the respect of this group, us kids included. I have the habit of calling him a cop, and I catch myself. It is not proper for a kid to disrespect any grown-up, and it is double disrespect when the grown-up is an official. I remember when I told my father, "The reason I call him a cop is because he is such a jerk. He tattle-tales to you anytime we do anything he doesn't approve." My father immediately demoted my "reason" to an "excuse," and I won't make the mistake of saying that out loud ever again!

"When he tells your folks what you've been up to, he is doing the job he is paid to do, not being a tattle tale," Doc Bucky says that a policeman has a tough job with hours of boredom interrupted by moments of sheer terror. If Doc Bucky says it, it must be true, so I gotta focus and stop calling him "cop." Okay? Okay.

"Mary Clare!"

"What? Oh! I was busy talking to myself, and didn't hear you call my name. Please go ahead, Johnnie T, tell us what you are doing in possession of Frank's gloves." I turned to give him my best "and this better be good" look.

He returned my look with a dingy-dangy smart-alecky smile! "Frank said you were sharp, Mary Clare—for a girl."

Little C yanked my braid to stop my—well, going off like a black cat, which is a small, short-fused firecracker.

"Whoa! Whoa! I apologize. Sit back down, please. Let me tell this story all the way through, and I'll answer any questions afterwards. I promise."

With a bottle of Coca-Cola in front of me, and three chocolate chip cookies, I centered my pencil over my note-taking-tablet and prepared for his story.

"Me and Frank—Frank and I..." he choked, coughed, took a sip of Coke, and started over, "This go-round started several years ago. My folks up in Lakefield, Minnesota signed papers so I could enlist early. I was only a couple three years older than some of you kids. My life up to then was 'the attitude.' I was convinced the world was against me, and I fought everyone about everything trying to prove I had the better answer to any and all problems. I wouldn't tolerate pity, and I thought any help offered was charity. I was so bad about accepting anything you couldn't give me the time of day."

Wow! What a great line. I made a mental note to use that for my own "attitude" attitude, and underlined it on my tablet.

He went on, "The idea of someone helping without a price or a hidden agenda just didn't register with me. Studying wasn't my idea of living, so rather than have me flunk out of school, and my parents knew I would fight workin' the farm, my folks signed the papers, and I went right into the Army. It didn't take no time for me to get through basic training and land in the back half of the Korean War. You kids are studying the Korean War in your history books. I lived what you are reading. When I hit Korea, the war was still going hot and heavy. Everyone knew the politicians were negotiating an end, but we soldiers were still fighting, getting hurt, and dying in that beautiful country that war had shot all to—well, I grew up knowing Minnesota cold, but it took that Korean winter to teach me about real cold. That winter in Korea messed up my internal temperature gauge. I'm a walkin', talkin', shiverin' case of brain freeze. That's why I live in South Texas now."

The mayor interrupted, "Anyone in need? It's ok to go to the bathroom or get another pop, as long as you do it quietly."

I think that gave Johnnie T the clue to get on with his story about meeting Frank.

"Anyway, my outfit was hunkered down trying to survive on top of a hill we had taken for the third time. Incoming mortar fire was brutal; we had flares up trying to see the enemy, the bad guys, before they could overrun our position. We were tired, getting low on ammunition, hungry—you kids can't imagine what the combination of cold, tired, hungry and no bullets can do to your attitude. I was curled up as tight as I could curl trying to keep my parts warm and still watch the hillside when all h-e-double-popsicle-sticks broke loose. Bullets flying everywhere, guys yelling for bullets or the medic, wind blowing the snow across the ridge, and I found out you could be in hell without any fire and brimstone. Then it got quiet!"

Quiet! I looked around and everyone, including the mayor, was sitting like a statue. Some of the Meanderthallers sat with a mouthful of cookie forgetting to chew and swallow.

"Just like that! Blasting noise one heart beat, and dead silence the next. I looked around at the other guys looking around, trying to see if everybody made it. It caught me by surprise when somebody grabbed the hood of my parka and started dragging me out of the foxhole. Whoever it was bounced me across some pretty rough hillside into the medics' first aid tent. Three of my buddies looked at me. They were wounded, and they looked to see where I got shot. I didn't feel nothin'. It took a couple minutes for me to realize that I couldn't feel anything, and I still thought sleep would be a suitable solution. Remember, I told you how cold and tired and cold and sleepy and cold I felt?

The Meanderthallers chorused: "NO!"

"No sleep when you are that cold."

"You can die of hy—hyper—no!—hypo—"

"Hypothermia!" Doc Bucky stood in the Town Hall hall doorway. "Hi, Johnnie T. Sorry I'm late. Have I missed much?"

The mayor shoved a mug of coffee toward the empty chair on the other side of Johnnie T. "Park it, Doc. Johnnie T was just laying the groundwork."

"Hi, Doc Bucky. Sure good to see you again. I haven't seen all you all since you used to dance in my folks stock barn hay loft."

Little C couldn't get to my braid in time as I blurted out "You're Johnnie T from the Tolly Barn family! My folks used to play there. How—" The cold stares of everyone but Johnnie T shut me up like a steel trap mid-question.

Johnnie T put his Coke down and continued. "I was just telling about the cold hillside, getting shot, somebody draggin' me out of the fox hole, and bouncing me on my backside to the aid station. My body was so cold there was no blood, until they trucked me down to the Mash Unit, and piled warm blankets under, over and around me. Guess this had happened before, because they had this really cute red-haired nurse assigned to taking my temperature, and trying to find my pulses. When I finally warmed up enough to bleed, they saw the blankets turning red, and next thing I was on a stretcher with this old character holding my hand as they headed me for surgery. He introduced himself, and apologized for the rough ride from the fox hole to the aid station.

Then he put on a gown, a surgical mask, and gloves and worked as the surgeon's assistant. When I woke up, I still had all my parts—well, two arms and two legs. The bullet had gone clean through my shoulder and out my back without destroying anything major."

"A hero! A real live hero with a bullet wound n' scars n' all." Actress-in-training Nancy was on her feet, applauding. Janie pulled her back down and handed her a cold pop.

"At least that's what they thought, until my temperature climbed and they had to go back into my chest. One rinky dinky piece of metal had sliced into the back of my lung, and it didn't cause trouble until I warmed up, had the shoulder surgery and started taking deep breaths. That's when the lung collapsed. They were going to ship me further up the health care line, but I begged to stay and recover in the Mash Unit. I wanted to hurry up 'n get well enough to help finish the fight with my buddies. None of that Purple-Heart-free-pass-home malarkey for me."

Now all the Meanderthallers were doing a low level cheer. "Bullet wound. Scars. Purple Heart." The chorus modified a football cheer. But what about Frank?

"That's when that old character who saved my life by dragging me out of the fox hole and then attending at my surgery turned into another kind of character. He started spending time at my cot. His visiting turned me in a different direction, a change in attitude, an approach to living I had never ever considered.

The Meanderthallers chorused: "A Bible-thumpin'-holy-roller in Korea? Are you kidding?"

Johnnie T took a chug of Coke and continued as though we had not interrupted him. "Frank—"

"Our Frank? Our Frank saved your life in Korea?"

"You knew our Frank before he came here?"

"Frank was a Bible-thumpin'-holy-roller?" The Meanderthaller chorus was on a roll.

"If you want the whole story, kids, you'll have to hold onto your guesses and give Johnnie T the floor. How 'bout if we take a break. Everybody stand up and stretch." The mayor signaled the policeman to bring another tray of cookies.

Each of us Meanderthallers said a thank-you, and smiled as the policeman served us cookies. He almost dropped the tray.

Chapter Nine

FRANK IN KOREA

After a short stand-up stretch, and armed with fresh cookies, we prepared to hear the rest of Johnnie T's story about knowing our Frank in Korea.

Johnnie cleared his throat and continued, "Frank turned out to be the MASH Unit spook!"

The grown-ups joined the Meanderthaller chorus of, "Ooooooo! Wow! Who'd a thunk it?" at this pronouncement. Little C and Melvin looked puzzled, so I leaned over, and whispered, "Spook is another word for spy." Johnnie T sat there waiting for the buzz to stop.

"Not everyone in the unit figured Frank out, but I did after that cute, red-haired nurse clued me in. She was sharp, and I was the first person who believed her hunch might be right. We watched, and sure 'nuff, every so often, Frank would get orders to go to Seoul for special training. He'd be gone for a week or so, then come back to the MASH Unit and work as whatever until the next 'training session.' When I would try to ask anyone about him, who he was, where he came from or anything about the man, nobody knew nothin'. I had to listen to lots and lots of gossip and rumors, plus absorb a lot of jealousy and anger at Frank before anything close to a whole picture appeared. It helped that I made friends with the MASH Unit clerk who 'unofficially' let me look at Frank's personnel file.

"It took awhile, but I found out Frank had been born in Singapore after his folks escaped one of those provinces in Russia. As a kid, he learned so many languages and dialects; I don't think he had a native language. As a young man, his father's family in America sponsored Frank, and he landed in New York City. He graduated from New York City University with a whole alphabet of initials after his name."

I whispered to Little C and Melvin, "Frank had a lot of documented smarts and degrees and initials after his name."

"The State Department recruited him, but no one knew exactly which branch of what department he answered to. His MASH job description said he was a medic, trained at the Fort Sam Houston, Texas, School of Paramedic Training. Most of the guys and gals of the MASH Unit thought he was an interesting old man serving out his years, until he could retire with a pension. They didn't think anything about his ability to talk with the North Korean gooks—I shouldn't use that word—it's the common slang word for an uncommon enemy soldier. Frank could communicate with any enemy soldier who landed wounded at our MASH Unit. If the MASH staff thought anything, it was to tag the ability to communicate as 'lucky,' or maybe there was jealousy, or anger at him for treating those enemy soldiers as human.

"That red-haired nurse and I figured out Frank's trips to Seoul meant the State Department knew that some Chinese or Russian advisor had defected, and Frank was tapped to either be the interpreter or 'accidentally' be put in the same cell as a defector having a similar legal problem. Frank became the inside man, getting information. With his dark skin and ability to speak any language, Frank was accepted for what he wasn't by the defector. Something must have gone wrong 'cause Frank never returned from one of those Seoul trips. We were so busy staying alive, and trying to keep other soldiers alive, that the war was over before we had time to search for him. There was no trace, no trail to follow, so I had to consider him lost, and try to hang on to the lessons he had taught me."

The mayor got up to get the coffee pot and pointed a finger at the still full pop machine so we took a quick break, but nobody left. Johnnie T could tell a great story, and we were too busy listening to question his veracity—that's another word for truth. I set out another pencil for taking notes. No way could I risk having a pencil break and be left without a way to keep notes.

"Nobody missed Frank more than me!" Johnnie T continued, "That old man took the time to set me on a whole different track. Nobody had ever made time to listen to anything I had to say. Really listen. When I was talking, Frank didn't interrupt or read a magazine. If he said anything, it was to drop a hint or slip in a suggestion, and let me keep talking. I was on the high that comes from finding out someone thinks you have value. Later, at night, I would remember his hint, and I'd begin to work it into my thinking and behaving. Okay. Example: School! I told Frank my folks signed me into the service early 'cause I hated school. He just listened, and then did two things: He convinced me I had a good brain, and offered to help me exercise it. Boy! Did he help me exercise it. He dug up books and made me read. He really didn't have to push me; the books he brought me were gooood. Like Macbeth by that Shakespeare guy; that story makes most families look like saints. And math? He'd hand me a problem, and help me figure through to the answer. He didn't use words like algebra or calculus; he helped me see the logical path to an answer. Same with language; he didn't know Spanish, so we learned it together.

"He complimented me when I would do little things that my momma had tried to pound into me as a kid, like hold a door open, or clean up a tray somebody left. I got to opening doors for people with their arms full of supplies, or grabbing a tray when there was an incoming wounded call, or go by and hold the hand of some poor soldier shot all to h—shot up bad. I didn't preach, or push the God thing; I'd just sit, hold his hand, and be there. Being alone is worse than bad at a time like that, and I remembered how I felt after surgery.

"It took a while to realize I felt good; the 'thanks,' the looks of surprise and gratitude were honest. And sleep! I was sleeping peacefully in the middle of that he—uh—war. Frank was the absolute slickest at turning me around. The selfish 'it's all about me and what I should have' attitude melted. I got to feeling good about making a difference for someone else, in little things that don't mean nothin' until you see the look on the face of a nurse with her arms full of surgical supplies, able to walk through that suddenly open door, or wipe the tears from a kid just as scared as I was and letting him know he was not alone. I really got a high from helping. Then Frank gave me the greatest gift: he convinced me I could 'spend' that gift of making a difference as long as I didn't do it for show, for credit, for an ulterior motive or expect a pay back. Let people say thanks, but insist they pass it on rather than try to pay it back.

"Since Frank's disappearance, I have tried to live that life of no-count giving. It's no big deal to give of time, of energy, of self, and of money. It's no big deal, but it is the very biggest deal when you live it."

"And Frank was very, very proud of you, Johnnie T." Mr. LaFloy stood in the kitchen doorway with my mother.

Johnnie T jumped up and ran at my mother with both arms open wide.

"JIM! Oh Jim, you are alive! And you look well. Promise you'll play 'Beyond the Reef' for me one more time before I die!" He took my mother by the arm and escorted her to the chair next to him—the chair just vacated by Doc Bucky, who chair-hopped one space to the right.

Mr. LaFloy parked in the chair next to Doc Bucky and continued "Hearing you talk about Frank's approach to living a rewarding life, I am reminded of a book written a few years ago that was made into a movie. The theme was identical to Frank's, and it makes no never mind who thought of it first. The point is that the life you are living affects those you encounter. You have the heart of *Magnificent Obsession* down, just as Lloyd Douglas wrote it. If you don't know the book, I have a feeling Frank did."

Then Mr. LaFloy added, "Okay. Mary Clare, before Little C pulls your pigtail braid off, let's have Johnnie T explain how he came by Frank's gloves."

Johnnie T took a deep breath, held it, and let it come out as a long sigh.

"My mother was sick, and she asked me to come visit one more time before she died. When I got to Lakefield, and saw how sick she was, I had to stay until she died. Dad and I grew to respect each other over those last weeks of her illness. He seemed proud of the man I was becoming, and my last memory of him is a hug—the one and only time we hugged. It was not his way, but I needed that memory, so I hugged him—and he hugged me back.

"It was my plan to catch a ride with a long-haul 18 wheeler truck headed for Texas. No sense wasting money on a plane ticket, and the trip cross country would give me time to think. I caught a ride with the local sheriff to the Iowa state line, and he asked your sheriff to give me a ride to the Terrell Truck Stop. The Cole-Anders Livestock folks run out of there, and I was hoping to find one of them headed south. When I walked into the truck stop, it was easy to pass the word that I was lookin' for a ride, so I just parked myself at the counter and started working on a cup of coffee. Somebody called my whole name! Now, nobody knows my whole name 'cepting my folks and a very few friends, so I almost choked on that coffee before I could look-see who knew me that well.

"Frank! It was Frank, wasn't it?" from the Meanderthallers.

"In the flesh! There stood that saint from the hell year of my life, alive and full of joy. We hugged and danced around like a couple kids until the waitress made us settle down. I grabbed my coffee, Frank ordered hot tea like he always did, and we retreated to a booth. We had lots of catchin' up to do starting with that last 'training run' to Seoul. He said they put him in a cell with a Chinese defector to find out if the guy was for real or a double agent. Turned out the guy was serious about defecting to our side to gain legal access to the United States. He claimed diplomatic immunity and was in danger for his life if the wrong North Koreans got him. The true-truth came out in that cell with Frank. He was an officer in a Chinese tong—that's a tough, illegal-drug dealing gang. The tong planned for him to be their front man, planting cells in United States cities. Frank established a friendship with that defector and with the State Department's encouragement was feeding valuable information to the Feds—until some total skunk ratted on Frank's true identity as a double agent."

"Who would be a traitor to our country?"

"Why would anyone put Frank in danger?"

"What a dirty rotten stinky-puddy-tat!" It was a quick explosion of energy, and then the Meanderthallers went back to listening with every brain cell.

"Frank thought it was one of the prison guards with a drug problem. The Chinese tong may have been supporting the guard's heroin habit, knowing addiction would make him totally indebted to them. When you are hooked on drugs, there is nothing more important than the next 'fix.' Loyalty to your country or friends scores a distant second to maintaining your drug supply.

"The Feds yanked Frank out of Korea into a witness protection program. They promised to hide him where ever he wanted until whatever time it would be safe for him to surface again. Location was his choice. Frank remembered me talking about Minnesota, but the towns were too small or too large. Then he spotted this town. Y'all are south of a big resort area with spots he could slip in and out of. You're located on a railroad line with big terminals connecting other rail lines within easy reach. Every so often, he would hop a freight and connect with a big city. When we met in the truck stop, he had gone to Kansas City to hear the opera *Carmen*, and somewhere on that trip, he was spotted. He had a feeling that someone had recognized him, maybe at the Opera, or it might have been while he was sharing Slum Gullion Stew in the Hobo Jungle of north K.C. It could have been an old vet from Korea days who dropped a dime on him.

Little C had that puzzled look again. So I leaned over and whispered, "Drop a dime means someone put a dime in a pay phone to make a phone call, maybe to the tong."

"Frank caught freight trains and switched as often as he could, but he wasn't sure he had shaken the tail."

Little C leaned close, and I heard Melvin explain *tail* as someone trying to follow Frank without Frank knowing they were there. Little C nodded.

The sheriff and I locked eyes but didn't interrupt. I could tell we both figured some skunk ratted Frank to the branch of a Chinese tong just getting active in Kansas City. I had read about that tong in the Des Moines newspaper. That could explain the four goons, too. The sheriff nodded; I knew we would talk later. Now, it was Johnnie T time.

"Frank had stepped off the Burlington Northern freight in Spencer, walked up to the Terrell Truck Stop, and there I was. We buried ourselves in a back booth to catch up on news. The waitress kept my coffee cup full, and Frank kept asking for more hot water for his tea bags. Frank was Frank—listening, asking questions, and interested in how life was happening for me. But this time it worked both ways. I had learned to listen, ask questions, and probe for information from the master, so I turned the conversation around.

"That's how I knew about you Meanderthallers and the other happenings here and at the Lakes. You Meanderthallers made Frank's life worth living in this self-imposed exile from the world. If it had not been for your questions, your enthusiasm for learning, but mostly, your love for a dark-skinned old scoundrel, he would have gotten old and quit long ago. Thanks kids! Thanks for what you meant for our friend."

Bang! There was that word again: scoundrel! But now was not the time to get distracted. I tuned back into the Johnnie T saga.

"We would still be talking if one of the Cole-Ander drivers hadn't walked over and asked if I was the kid who wanted a ride to Texas. I made a quick run to the men's room, and came back to the booth for one more hug before heading out the door with that trucker. It must have been during my trip to the men's room that Frank slipped these leather fur-lined gloves into the pocket of my blast jacket. When I got home to San Antonio, I called up here to talk with 'anyone, someone, whoever' would tell Frank I got home safe, and get an address to mail his gloves back to him. That's when I found out Frank was dead. I booked the next flight up, and this state patrolman gave me a ride here."

We sat dazed with information overload. I had heard that phrase old scoundrel, but my brain was too overloaded to recall when or where. Old scoundrel! Old scoundrel! My brain was on tape delay; I would have to circle around later.

It was getting on toward supper time, so the mayor adjourned the meeting. Johnnie T agreed to spend the night in Mr. LaFloy's basement apartment, and we Meanderthallers invited him for a Green Mountain at the drug store soda fountain after school the next day. The mayor and the policeman headed for the kitchen, with the used coffee cups. All the Meanderthallers put our pop bottles in the empties rack. Mother and I were just about to the door when I heard my name called.

"Mary Clare,"

I turned to see what Johnnie T wanted.

He stood with Frank's gloves extended. "I think Frank would want you to have these." My eyes went from Johnnie T's face to the hand that held Frank's gloves. It was clear he meant what he said: Frank's gloves would be mine. All I had to do was reach out and accept them.

Me! Accept a gift? I was a giver, but nobody could give me anything. Like a dropped rock, I remembered Johnnie T telling about his attitude when he was a kid. Yeah. I remember that line: "you couldn't give me the time of day." Johnnie T just stood there watching me work through a dilemma he remembered well. He smiled that dingy-dangy smile, winked and walked over to take my hand. He put Frank's gloves in my hand, patted my head, and walked away. He understood!

Mother and I looked at the fine leather, and I had her slide her gifted musician's hands in the gloves. She flexed her hands, and stroked her cheeks, and then my cheeks, with the softest leather either of us had ever felt. As she slid her hands free, she stopped to look closely at the back of the left hand glove.

"There's something inside this glove. Let's get in good light, and study how to get whatever is in there out, without damaging this wonderful leather."

We found a window with direct sun light. With her eagle eyes, Mother located the seam between leather and fur. She identified the thread as being a recent addition, which she felt confident she could remove without damage to either the fur or the leather. From her purse, she extracted her trusty Mother-of-Pearl handled pocket knife, and ever sooooo carefully, cut the threads until she could use her tweezers to reach inside. Out came a business-card-sized piece of paper with penciled words: "Last Will: greentt2mc2kpcbn2nwtch.ftlkr2jt. Frank Hashianski"

"Frank was right, Mary Clare. You are a remarkable girl and so is Jim." Johnnie T stood looking over my mother's shoulder at the little card.

I grabbed the card and the gloves as I ran for the door. The grown-ups might have wanted to talk, but it was all too much for me.

It was too late in the day to do anything but go home. In the safety of the 'girls' dorm', where my bed stood between my older sister Gee's bed and my younger sister Little C's bed, I was safe. I sure didn't want to talk to anybody until I had time to think some things through. What can't I remember about scoundrel? And now the little card with all that code. Yee cats and little doglets!

I heard Mother come home to fix supper before she got dressed for a job at Vacation Village. She didn't ask me to come help; I went out and set the table on my own. She patted my shoulder but didn't say a word. I told you my mother was a cool person!

Chapter Ten

THE CODE CARD…AND A TATTOO

By the next day, I had the beginnings of a plan. Immediately after school, the Meanderthallers were parked in the soda fountain back booth, and I was at the store front door waiting for Johnnie T. He was on time, accepted the offer of a Green Mountain, and slid into the back booth between Little C and me. The Meanderthallers were on their good manners for a new record of three minutes before we started bombarding Johnnie T with questions.

"Could we see the scar from the bullet wound?"

"Did you have to shoot anyone in Korea?"

"Do you still like to go hunting or are you 'off' guns?"

"Would you talk some Spanish for us?"

"Do you think Frank was tailed from Kansas City?"

"Do you believe Frank was murdered or do you side with the rest of the grown-ups?"

"Will you help us track down the killers?

The Meanderthaller chorus was firing off questions without giving Johnnie T a chance to answer. He tasted his Green Mountain, waiting for us to run down. He didn't use a sissy straw; he drank his Green Mountain right from the glass like some of us did.

"Okay. Okay. If you all are ready for answers, I'm ready to try. Yes, you can see my scar but not right here or now. Yes. I had to kill people in Korea. I didn't have much of a choice. It was me shooting them or them shooting me. I still love to go hunting for sport and the meat. I shot a triple in pheasants with my dad's Ithaca Model 37 12 gauge pump while I was in Lakefield. Mom was still well enough to cook them, and it was the best pan-fried pheasant and the tastiest pheasant noodle soup I'll ever eat. Esta comida muy ricoh! That was very good food. Yes! I think Frank's death is suspicious. Like I said, he was the MASH Unit spook. A spook—a spy—is more. More than you see. More than his papers say. More than his job description describes. And he made more enemies just being so mysterious."

The Meanderthallers sat with wide eyes, suspended mugs, and total concentration waiting for Johnnie T to continue.

"War makes strangers out of people. In war, you don't get close to anyone because they might get shot next patrol. You don't let anyone in 'cause this is war, and they might not recall incidents the same way when the war is over—if they live. Everyone ends up suspicious of everyone else because the bullet that should be going at an enemy soldier may end up in you; it's called "friendly fire." That means someone on your side shoots at someone else on your side; the other word for that is *fragging*. Frank must have been the target of more than one attempt to get even for some real or imagined snub. I overheard more than one Mash Unit person make a nasty crack about Frank getting another cushy trip to Seoul for more special training. They didn't want to know Frank was a valuable person. All they cared about was that Frank got a trip to Seoul, and they didn't.

"He was always trying to help us wounded warriors, but very few of us made that decision to change. And more than one who tried 'no-count living' threw it away 'cause it didn't give immediate rewards. And there were always easier ways to survive the pain, or the war, or the prospect of going back up another hill. I'm talking 'dope', drugs, white powder, or 'weed.' Frank could get really, really down when one of us chose to be a dope-head. He took it as a personal loss.

"I don't think Frank realized how dangerous it was to rescue one of his fallen warriors. The guys dealing or doing dope were working for some very bad people. Every customer those 'baddies' lost to Frank cost them money. They didn't care for the life of a soldier; their god was dope and money. Frank was their enemy. When I would try to tell him to back off, let go, rescue someone who wanted to be rescued, he would just look at me and remind me how far I had come, but I had never been on drugs. He would wade right back into that dopey world. It would be very possible for one of those old veterans from Korea to have spotted Frank; they would drop a dime on him in a minute. Anger, hatred, jealousy and drugs will make a man do crazy things."

Little C looked at me with a "Huh?" all over her face. I leaned over and whispered: "Remember? Drop a dime means someone put a dime in a pay phone and made a phone call."

"So Frank's fall off the trestle could have been a murder committed by someone connected with the Kansas City tong, someone from the Korea days, or...or...or... Remember, we still haven't ID'd the goons who tried to get in Frank's room at the Komfy Kozy Kave-inn." Johnnie T. shrugged his shoulders and looked overwhelmed. Little C scrambled to her feet and hugged Johnnie T around the neck. None of us said anything about standing on the booth leather with her shoes.

"Johnnie T and fellow Meanderthallers, may I please have your undivided attention." My words hit the air waves like a tornado. Talk about captivating an audience. Herm was so startled, he tipped over his root beer float. Everybody grabbed napkins to control the runoff and piled the wet mess in the empty mug.

"Yesterday my mom found a coded message in the back of Frank's left hand glove. This morning I hand-made exact copies; one for each of you:

Last Will: greentt2mc2kpcbn2nwtch.ftlkr2jt.—Frank Hashianski

Please take a pencil, and use whatever time you need, to decode this message. Try to make sense of these initials, and if you get stuck, just jot down words that might fit. Please work quietly, individually, without talking or sharing. It will be interesting to see how many of us reach the same message. Start now while I go order a second round of Root Beers, Nehi Orange Sodas, Cokes, and Green Mountains."

Johnnie T acknowledged my attempt to sound official with one of his dingy-dangy grins. Every head bowed, and pencils started squeaking across the papers as I went up to the soda fountain where Mrs. Murrey was playing soda jerk. I visited with her about her poodle before placing the order for refills. She brought the tray just as the last Meanderthaller pencil hit the booth top. Everyone reached for their refill and took that first sip. I gathered the sheaf of papers and started reading the decodings of: Last Will:greentt2mc2kpcbn2nwtch.ftlkr2jt. Frank Hashianski.

"Amazing! Everyone of you reached the same solution I did except for the very first series of letters. Johnnie T, please help. Here's the consensus of what we think Frank put on that little card."

He studied the papers spread across the booth table top. Johnnie T frowned. "Mary Clare and Meanderthallers, I agree: this is Frank's last will. The first word is green but we'll have to work on the two t's."

The Meanderthallers had scribbled lots of t words, but nothing went together or made logical connection. Then my mental light bulb went on.

"Tea! Johnnie T, you said Frank always drank tea. So that would make the first bunch of letters green tea but what could the second t be?" I had lost sleep trying to break those t's into something, and it was there all the time.

Johnnie T had that dingy-dangy, smart-aleck grin, so I wasn't surprised when he had the answer.

"Tin. Green tea tin. The number 2 stands for the word to mc—that's you, Mary Clare. Green tea tin to Mary Clare." Johnnie T was very pleased with himself.

"We all guessed cbn must be cabin, and that goes to Mary Clare 2. Figure the number 2 is code for too, nwtch means and his pocket watch. I'll guess Frank will have to come back from death to explain what cabin. He might have meant carbine or ship cabin or cabinet. We'll have to have more information to clear up that code word."

Boy! Did I have to work at keeping my mouth closed. So, Frank knew I knew about his cabin hide-out, but I just didn't feel this was the time or place to say anything. As close as the Meanderthallers were to me, I was still locked in that respect for privacy mode. There would be a right time to share about the cabin, and I would know when that time was—whenever it was. I raced on to the next bunch of letters. "Johnnie T, I think it is clear that Frank wanted you to have his footlocker, and I'm sure that should include all the books, papers and music. Agreed?"

With one voice the Meanderthallers agreed.

I continued. "Next order of business is Frank's last name: Hashianski! At last he has a full name."

Johnnie T didn't say it, but I realized he would have known Frank's last name from the time in Korea. A little red light went on in the back of my brain. I felt it, but it would take time to figure out why that bothered me.

"Let's call the sheriff and share the note—er—Last Will with him and get his advice on what to do next as far as legalities go. He will also know where your footlocker is, Johnnie T. Will you let us go through Frank's stuff with you? My mom has a piece of music Frank wrote and gave her. Maybe there will be other things in there like my green tea tin." I watched Johnnie T's eyes as I said all that. He winked at me and added that dingy-dangy grin before agreeing.

The sheriff responded to our phone call with great interest and insisted we include the local policeman in our footlocker opening. We set the occasion for right after school; all of us were to meet at 3:30 in the Town Hall hall. The sheriff said he'd bring the foot locker. I was sure glad he volunteered to give the local policeman a heads-up. Knowing our policeman, he will spread the word to the Mayor and Doc Bucky and Mr. LaFloy. I'll tell mom. Then EJ, Little C, me, and our mom can make our own parade as we head for the meeting. It will be interesting to see if anyone else shows up invited-by-gossip.

It was too soon to leave the back booth, so we got to shooting the paper off the ends of fresh straws when quiet, never-nothing-to-say Jerry C asked, "Johnnie T, did you ever see Frank's tattoo?"

I exploded before Johnnie T could answer, "Tattoo? Where did you hear Frank had tattoos? Nobody in this town has a tattoo 'cepting Weird Warren. On his stomach he has a tattoo of his antique Chris Craft speed boat. Remember the time he arrived at the Milford vs. Mallard men's softball game and showed off his tattoo? The first shock was him coming to the game without a shirt, and then he started doin' waves with his stomach muscles. A bunch of the kids got sick watching that boat heave up and down. The mothers made Warren go put on a shirt, and quit making the kids sick. I just don't see Frank with a boat tattoo."

"Hey, put on your memory caps! Mr. LaFloy mentioned a tattoo and pictures sent to Washington at Frank's funeral." Melvin remembered what I forgot. The Meanderthallers nodded, and Jerry C continued,

"My pop saw the tattoo. Frank has a strange initial on his left arm. It is an H with a diamond design on top. It reminded my pop of the tattoos WW II prisoners in the concentration camps wore. I told him we saw pictures in Show 'n Tell of the tattoos Marvin Leritzki's Grandma has. I'll never forget the picture taken of her bony arm when she was liberated from that terrible camp. My pop says the tattoo on Frank's arm was sorta like that."

Being center of attention was new to Jerry C, so we had to encourage him to keep talking.

"The county coroner who would normally do the autopsy on a dead person was in Minnesota ice fishing for muskies. When they finally got him on the phone, he was having way too much fun fishing to interrupt his vacation to come do an autopsy on a dark-skinned old man who most likely just fell off the trestle. He told Doc Bucky to go ahead and do the autopsy and to have somebody who wouldn't get sick or faint write down anything interesting.

"Yuck! Who would want to watch somebody cut into somebody?" The chorus couldn't stand the thought.

"My pop, you all know he works in the meat market at Jacobsen Grocery and General Store. He's used to blood, so Doc Bucky asked him to be there. Mr. LaFloy was there, too. Pop said there were real bad scars on Frank's body from being whipped or bad beat up. His feet were all bent up, and his toes were curled almost under. Doc Bucky said that might a' been from fever as a kid or being forced to work without shoes or boots."

I spoke up with a brilliant deduction. "No wonder Frank always wore long sleeved shirts and sturdy working boots."

We Meanderthallers waited as quiet, never-say-nothing Jerry C accepted a Nehi Orange, took a long drink, and continued.

"Doc Bucky noticed Frank's left hand was clenched tight around something. Mr. LaFloy thought Frank had just made a fist like he was fixing to hit somebody, but Doc Bucky was sure Frank was holding onto something. Doc Bucky was so sure he was right, and Mr. LaFloy was so sure Doc was wrong, they bet a twenty-dollar bill."

As Jerry C reached for the Nehi Orange, the Meanderthaller chorus demanded, "Who won? How did they figure out who won?"

"Doc Bucky has an x ray machine so he took a picture of Frank's hand. Sure enough, there it was."

"What? What was it? Tell us, or there'll be no more Nehi Orange!" hissed out of the chorus. Hissed because we wanted to know, but we didn't want to draw attention.

"It was the pocket watch and chain that Frank kept his goldstone heart on. The watch and chain and goldstone heart were stuck in Frank's hand so tight, Doc had to do surgery to get it out in one piece."

I bit my lip till it bled trying to keep my mouth shut and my words choked in. Half of Frank's goldstone heart, at least I thought it was half of Frank's goldstone heart, was in my jeans pocket right where I put it. Remember, I told you I happened to see it glisten in the No Name Creek water as Frank's body was skidded up the creek bank. I just picked it up, and dropped it in my pocket. But it was only half of a goldstone heart. I'll think about where the other half could be and who else had a goldstone heart later after Jerry C finishes this story.

"Doc Bucky took to studying the pocket watch and found the way to open the back. There was that same H with a diamond. The back of the watch matches the tattoo on his arm."

So? So? We were frowning and grimacing trying to figure. So? So what?

"Mr. LaFloy made a drawing of what was on the pocket watch back. He has a friend who works in Washington D.C. for one of those government places. A copy of the drawing and a picture of Frank's arm with the tattoo were air-mailed to Washington, and now we wait for word.

"Wait! Wait! Didn't they think of ol' Mose?" The question came from Little C. My little blue eyed blonde sister could come up with some doozies, and this was a doozy. We could all picture ol' Mose, the patient old man with the gi-normous nose. He was a WWI veteran who survived small pox; it was the small pox that put those bad scars on his face and big nose, and he could speak three or four foreign languages. We kids treated him with the respect due a living treasure, but we were too intimidated to make friends with him. I sure would have liked to have heard him and Frank talk history. Just think of the history they knew first hand 'cause they lived through it.

Jerry C spoke right up. "Yeah, Mr. LaFloy, my pop, the sheriff, and Doc Bucky piled in Doc's big Buick and drove down to ol' Mose's trailer. Ol' Mose invited them in. The place is so small it got crowded in a hurry. Doc Bucky explained why they were there and my pop said ol' Mose's eyes got bigger 'n bigger. When ol' Mose actually looked at the picture of the tattoo and then saw the back of the watch, my pop said he almost fainted. He dropped the pictures and shook his head back and forth before backing out of the trailer. Last they saw, he disappeared down the road toward No Name Creek."

That's when it hit me. Last summer I was meandering along the edge of the old gravel pit where it butts up against No Name Creek when a flash of light on the trestle caught my eye. I was half a mile away, and my eyes can't focus at that distance, but I am pretty sure it was Frank and ol' Mose sitting with their legs dangling off the edge of the trestle. Whatever they were handling was giving off that flash of light, like a reflection off a watch. By the time I drifted the half a mile to the trestle, they were gone, and I plumb forgot the incident till now. When my brain circled back around to the meeting, Jerry C was working on a fresh Nehi Orange and was promising to let us all know if and when there was a reply from Washington D.C.

We had all had it for the day. It helped that my dad opened the door just then and came in the drug store. Like a covey of quail spooked by a fox, we scattered and headed for home. I don't know which way Johnnie T went.

Chapter Eleven

FRANK'S FOOT LOCKER

It was Thursday afternoon, Doc Bucky's usual afternoon off, but he came barreling around the corner in his big Buick to park behind his office. By the time the Buick door slammed shut, Doc was across the empty lot, double timing into the Town Hall to join the group waiting for the sheriff to bring Frank's foot locker. The local policeman had coffee ready for the grown- ups, cold pop in the cooler for us Meanderthallers, and the Mayor's wife had brought home-made cookies. Johnnie T was sitting next to my mother as she played on the Town Hall hall piano. Her ramrod-straight back next to his young man slouch lasted until Doc Bucky grabbed his collar and sat him up straight. Then it turned into a regular song fest with Doc Bucky, Mr. LaFloy, and Johnnie T trying to remember the words to the tunes they were requesting. They couldn't stump Jim with their requests, and when they ran out of requests, she would start on a tune they hadn't remembered. It was one wonderful jam session that came to a halt when the sheriff rolled the foot locker into the room on a heavy duty dolly. The guys grabbed hold and lifted it up on a table.

It looked like one of those foot lockers every soldier had at the foot of his cot or bunk in the movies. Heavy duty metal with support boards and handles all painted in military green, but there was no stenciled name on this locker! Johnnie T lifted the lid, and we all stared at the orderly system inside. There were wooden slats supporting trays of stuff on top of more trays with more stuff. Johnnie T started lifting out the trays. Music books and more books lined up on the top tray. Next came a tray with neatly stacked tablets with Frank's hand writing. Was he writing a story or keeping a diary? I thought of asking Johnny T if I could read them when he is finished looking them over. There were several tablets with music notes and words. My mother latched onto those, and Johnnie T told her they were hers to keep.

"Hey, Doc Bucky! Here's something for you!" Everybody stopped to look at the totally unbelievably, gor-ge-mous wooden box Johnnie T lifted out of the locker. A piece of tablet paper across the lid had Doc Bucky printed on it. It was the box that caught everyone's attention. The wood had some kind of something to make the wood grains translucent—that means you could almost see through them. My Gran'pa would appreciate all the hours someone spent oiling and sanding the wood of that box. It was about the size of a piece of typing paper and four or five inches deep. There was an itty-bitty padlock on the delicate latch. Doc Bucky cradled the box and handed it toward my mother as though he knew she would treat it like the jewel it was.

"Use both hands, Jim. This is heavy for its size."

The sheriff put a chair where mother could sit and put the box on her lap. Her musician hands caressed the wood, and she looked closely at the padlock.

"Please don't break this lock. Maybe Jiggs, the jeweler, can somehow open this padlock." Ever the artist, my mother couldn't stand having such a thing of beauty damaged. Doc Bucky smiled, dug a soft leather coin purse out of his pocket and pulled a tiny key on a gold chain out of the coin purse.

"Here, Jim. Frank gave this to me on a Sunday morning several months ago. See if this fits."

Mother slipped the key in the padlock and—it worked! By now, everybody in the room was on point. Mother looked at Doc Bucky, and he nodded.

"Go head, Jim. Open it!"

Hearts! Goldstone hearts! Layers and layers of goldstone hearts on soft felt pads. Inside the lid was an envelope with the flap opened. Mother handed the paper inside to Doc Bucky.

"What a treasure! Names, dates, and a sentence or two in neat columns provide a history of the goldstone heart legacy." Doc Bucky shared the folded sheet inside the envelope, but I saw him tuck a 3 by 5 card in his shirt pocket. He glanced at Jim but didn't say anything right then. I'm going to remember not to forget to ask him about that 3 by 5 card later. Doc Bucky retrieved the list, folded and put it back in the envelope and then locked the box again.

"LaFloy, let's you and me talk about keeping the goldstone heart legacy going. It does a lot of good, and Frank will live on through these stones. We'll work out the details over coffee."

Mr. LaFloy nodded, and we all went back to Frank's foot locker. The trays with books were lined up on a long table. The sheriff took every book and leafed through it as though he expected to find something hidden in it. The policeman caught on and started helping check each book.

"Look careful, everybody. Remember Wilma Jean and Donnie's ma saw the first hundred-dollar bills in one of the music books on the top tray. They quit looking immediately to call the sheriff. Check each book careful like."

Now we were all opening each individual book and commenting on the titles and topics. The sheriff nudged our policeman.

"Aren't you glad we stopped looking for money at the first tray of music books? We would have been a week going through all these books one at a time." The books being examined now were from the lower trays. I think it was the policeman who found the book with the Green Tea Tin stashed in the hollowed out part. It was a Zane Grey western. Johnnie T reached for the tin, but the sheriff handed it directly to me.

"Wow! If you thought that wood box was beautiful, look at this, Mom!" Mother and I were studying the tin, admiring the fancy Chinese art work, the scrolling and strange printing when Johnnie T almost ordered, "Open it up and see what's so valuable that Frank left it to you in his will." Again that little red light went on in my brain!

I shook the tin to check for contents. Was it loose tea, tea bags, or something noisy? It was heavy and made a soft thud sound as I tilted it back and forth. Doc Bucky came out of the kitchen with a small empty dish where I could pour the contents. Everyone gathered around as I pried the lid off the Green Tea Tin. Carefully, I tilted the open tin over the saucer. Out came loose tea that smelled like spicy oranges, and a something made of felt. It was two pieces of thick felt that made a sandwich. I looked at Mother and she slid one hand under the "sandwich" and used her other hand to separate the pieces of it.

"Rocks! Mr. Frank gave me seven little rocks? But I will treasure them 'cause Mr. Frank gave them to me. Even if they are way too small for throwing."

Johnnie T went to pick them up, and Doc Bucky bumped him off balance.

"Hands off, Johnnie T. Those belong to Mary Clare! She may think those are little rocks, but we're going to ask the jeweler, Mr. Jiggs, to identify them exactly. I can see an opal, an amethyst, a pearl, amber—look, there is a complete preserved flea—and the other three I'm not sure of." Doc Bucky put his arm across my shoulders.

"Mary Clare, those seven little rocks will pay your way through college when you are ready to go. Those are very fine gem stones, and I would advise you to put them in the bank vault for awhile. Mr. Jiggs will come out of his jewelry store long enough to tell you exactly what a treasure you have in those seven little rocks." Doc Bucky and Mr. LaFloy both snickered at the thought of Mr. Jigg's face when he sees the seven little rocks. I didn't know grown-ups could snicker till I saw it.

Johnnie T looked like he had a sour ball jaw breaker in his mouth. He almost said something, stopped himself, almost said something, stopped himself, and after several almosts, he finally stepped away. He went back to the foot locker and continued lifting out trays. The policeman stood next to him, spreading things neatly out on the table. In the very bottom of the locker was an album the size that could have held newspaper clippings or stuff for a scrap book or pictures. Johnnie T picked it up and went over in the corner to check it out. He opened it and burst into tears. Everyone went to see what in the world had caused this cloud-burst. It was a photo album and more, much more. Frank had made a coded verbal and visual record of the people he had been able to "gift with the gift of no-count giving." There on the first page was a picture of the kid Johnnie T with bandages around his chest and shoulder. It was verbal and visual proof positive that Frank considered Johnnie T a genuine success story. Johnnie T sobbed until I thought he would surely run dry. Doc Bucky brought him a glass of cold water, and a towel with ice cubes, for the back of his neck. Nobody said anything until Johnnie T cried himself out. He sipped the cold water, used a big napkin to wipe the last tears, and after a couple false starts his voice kicked in.

"Mary Clare, I apologize. I planned this return trip with the idea of finding Frank's stash and keeping it for myself. Yeah. It entered my mind that I would be throwing away all the good things I was working to become, to revert back into that selfish, self-centered kid who caused my folks lots of heart aches. What a goof-ball! I guess slipping and being "human" is a life time problem. There is no way I could have lived with myself, and I know that now. Frank really did do a number on my head and heart with that 'no-count giving' plan."

He took a big swig of cold water.

"Thank you, kids. You, Meanderthallers. Y'all will forever be my guardian angels. All I'll have to do is look in my heart and y'all will be there. This is my crossroads. Right here. Right now. For the rest of my life, I deliberately choose the path less traveled, because it is the right path. I'll live proud of who I am. No one will know what all I do for others. It is only important that I do for others and get them to pass it on. I ask you to forgive me and believe me. Please."

The grown-ups clapped when we Meanderthallers charged Johnnie T for a group hug. Mother had rescued the seven little rocks in their felt-sandwich. They were carefully folded in one of her famous linen handkerchiefs, resting on her lap.

"Jim, let us walk you and Mary Clare to the bank right now." Mr. LaFloy and Doc Bucky accompanied us. The banker almost passed out when he saw the little rocks. He rushed us back into the vault. I have never seen the inside of a room with walls that thick. It was scary just to look at that door, and I was ready to get out as soon as we stepped in. The banker pulled out a little key, put it in the wall, pulled out a long tray that was really a drawer and made me put the rocks, in the felt sandwich, down in the drawer. He put it back in the wall, turned the key, and handed it to me.

"Mary Clare, your Mother will co-sign the safe deposit box, but you can come and look at them here in the vault anytime." The banker was still in shock at this whole Frank thing.

As we walked back to the Town Hall, I started talking.

"I'm going to learn how to care for those gor-ge-mous things. I'll have to come to the bank, get them out of that box long enough to do—whatever I have to do, as often as Mr. Jiggs says." I had to hurry to keep up with Mother, Doc Bucky and Mr. LaFloy and talk at the same time. "I'm too young to know what to do with those rocks. I'm really too young to appreciate them now, aren't I? They must have a heck of a history, and when I grow up, I'll embark on an odyssey to learn how Frank came to own them." Mother put an arm around my shoulders and gave me a little hug, which meant I was right-on, even if I did use a lot of words.

Back in the Town Hall hall, Doc Bucky rescued the wooden box with the goldstone hearts and headed for his big Buick. Mother put the music books and music stuff in our Radio Flyer wagon, and we headed for home. Everything else went back in Frank's, well, now Johnnie T's foot locker, and Johnnie T used the heavy-duty dolly to roll the foot locker out to Mr. LaFloy's pickup truck. They planned to park that locker in the corner of Mr. LaFloy's rec room. Just thinking of all the books still in that big foot locker gave me goose bumps. I hope Johnnie T will share. Maybe we could set up a library sign-out system, so us kids could read the books that Frank had read. If he thought enough of them `to keep them, we needed to learn what and why. And the tablets with Frank's writing, maybe Johnnie T and I could read 'em together. I couldn't see very far, very good, but I could see to read, and there's a lifetime of reading in that locker. I made myself a promise to get "schmart" before I got old.

Chapter Twelve

CLUES ADD UP

"Hey, kids! The mayor would like to see you in his office."

We heard the clack of the ice house door latch being slipped, so we were not surprised when Mr. Witerock's face appeared in the top half of the Dutch door. The Meanderthallers were cooling our heels and our behinds, on the loose straw of the ice house floor. We had been burning brain cells trying to put some kind of pattern to all the clues of the last couple days. It seemed like the more things we found out, the less we knew! The truth shouldn't be so hard to discover and uncover! Anyways, we picked ourselves up, dusted each other off, and headed up town to the Town Hall.

The mayor was in the Town Hall hall talking with Mr. LaFloy. They were waiting for us, and while they were waiting, they had prepared a really neat seating arrangement. They had put a half circle of folding chairs with two tables angled into a sorta kinda round table arrangement. The two men were working on coffee. The pop cooler was well stocked, and we helped ourselves; remembering to fold a napkin so the bottles wouldn't leave rings on the tables. We parked and waited; wondering what could be in that big, very official looking envelope in front of the Mayor. It didn't take long to find out.

Mr. LaFloy started right out. "Kids, this envelope just arrived from my friend at the Pentagon. It took some real snooping by my Pentagon contacts to track down the history of the tattoo on Frank's arm."

"Score zero for the snooping by professionals. Score a big one for Lady Luck." Doc Bucky stood laughing in the kitchen doorway, coffee mug in hand. He walked over and pulled out the chair next to Mr. LaFloy. "Go 'head, tell these kids how the best snoops in Washington couldn't identify the tattoo on Frank's arm or the drawing of the back of the watch.

"Doc is right. The professionals in the FBI, the National Intelligence Agency, the Pentagon, and who knows who else, had gone through their files with no results. Not one of our best government agencies could tell us, or each other, the significance of that H with the diamond design on top." Mr. LaFloy reached for his coffee mug.

The Meanderthallers had had it. We chorused, "So who knew?"

"Who could tell what that weird H and diamond symbol meant?"

"Do we know or not?"

"Doc is right about Lady Luck. Each of the agencies working to decode the tattoo had sent one of their agents to a 'let's compare notes' meeting. The snoops were on a coffee and donut break in the Pentagon cafeteria. They had the pictures of the tattoo spread out where everyone at the table could see. One of the Pentagon cafeteria waiters was refilling their water glasses, when he saw a picture of Frank's arm with the tattoo. He poured water all over the table, and almost dropped the pitcher, before someone could grab it–and him.

"Uncle Frank! Uncle Frank! Where is he? What happened? Somebody tell me why you have a picture of my Uncle Frank's arm!" came gushing out of that waiter.

The pro's gathered up the pictures, collared the waiter, and hustled him out of the cafeteria. They rushed upstairs to a conference room, where he could be filmed and recorded. They wanted a record of what this waiter could reveal. How could a common, garden-variety waiter identify in one glance what the best snoop organizations in the USA could not identify after all that research?

"In this envelope is a transcript of the waiter's testimony." Mr. LaFloy had the full attention of the Meanderthallers. "You can read the whole thing if you want. For the sake of time let me start by telling you the short version. Turns out Frank came from a family categorized as living treasure jewelry designers in their native country, similar to the Faberge family of Russia. I bet you have seen pictures of the jeweled eggs the Faberge family made for the Czar of Russia."

There was unison "Yes sir."

"Beautiful things."

"Gorgeous!"

"Absolutely gor-ge-mous!"

"When the government where the Hashianski family had lived for generations changed, and the new regime started persecuting the privileged class, Frank's father anticipated trouble. He tried to get permission to join a brother in the United States, but his request was denied. The family could not enter the country of choice, so they accepted the hospitality of Singapore. Shortly after arriving in Singapore, as the family was adjusting to a totally different life style, Frank was born. His father tattooed the family code or crest—that H with the diamond—on Frank's arm when he was a small child. The thinking was, if Frank was ever separated from the family, the tattoo would provide and verify his identity to people knowledgeable of the family.

The family tried to establish a legitimate jewelry business, fit into the social and scholastic framework of Singapore and become accepted in the community. Frank went to school, and was found to have a gift for music. Even as a child, he showed great promise at the piano and organ. But the local kids weren't tolerant of him as a person or as a student, and his outstanding musical ability was a cause for much jealousy. Frank was a small target who learned quickly about unobtrusive invisibility: see them first and evade rather than confront. When one of the rival jewelry-making families kidnapped Frank and almost tortured him to death trying to extract Hashianski family jewelry-making secrets, Frank escaped, and fled to his uncle in New York City. We know the story from there."

But we Meanderthallers were not satisfied. "Does the waiter know about us Meanderthallers?"

"Does he know how much we cared for Frank?"

"Did he know how Frank died?" The chorus was frantic.

"Would the family come, take Frank's body and move it where we couldn't go to the cemetery, and visit him?"

"We worked hard to uncover the truth, and we're not going to quit now! It isn't fair for strangers to have so much control over this situation."

"It just isn't fair, is it?"

Doc Bucky fielded our outburst, and I learned again how different yet similar kids and grown-ups think.

"You kids are growing up in church. You are in different places on Sunday, but you are all learning the same stories and the same rules. Instead of ordering you all to NOW HEAR THIS, I am asking you to listen and hear me as I share a very private story. You don't know that Frank and I would have a cup of tea in my office on most Sunday mornings. Nobody knew, and we didn't see the need to tell. Over a cup of tea, two men discovered brotherhood. We were from very different backgrounds, different lives, and different life-styles, very like and very unlike! Yet we found we had almost identical attitude toward belief in power greater than our own. Mary Clare, you wondered if Frank ever went to church. He never left church. To him church was people. How you treated people, what you could give without expecting pay back, whether you could sleep peacefully at night, and a general inner certainty that there was a Reason for things happening the way they did, even if what happened didn't make logical sense at the time."

The wide-eyed look in our eyes brought a response from Mr. LaFloy.

"No! You kids can't quit going to your church on Sunday, nor can you cut any classes or studies your folks suggest. You need to learn the ropes before you can climb the mountain. These years will provide you with chances to apply the rules you're supposed to be learning, to stumble and make mistakes, to learn your folks love you even when they seem like tough wardens.

"Keep the faith, and learn there are many names for the Power behind this world and a reason for what happens, even when it isn't fair! If you live long enough, you'll realize, as Doc and I do, that there is love for us poor fools making a mess of the world. We enjoy love and tolerance far beyond what we deserve. The word is grace. Remember Frank's 'no-count giving'? Use that system as a way of dealing with life. You can fuss about what isn't fair, or you can live without keeping score. Try behaving because you KNOW it is the right thing to do."

Doc Bucky added one more thought. "I want you kids to know Frank had a good heart for helping but a tired old heart for living. His fall from the trestle might have been due to a heart attack."

Melvin and I and EJ let out the same sound. It was a "NO!" a gasp and an explosion of "heart attack?"

"Crickety! I hadn't thought that thought."

We walked out of the Town Hall in silent shock. The knowledge about Frank took a back seat to the ideas Mr. LaFloy and Doc Bucky laid on us. We'll be thinking on all those thoughts for a while to come—most likely the rest of our lives.

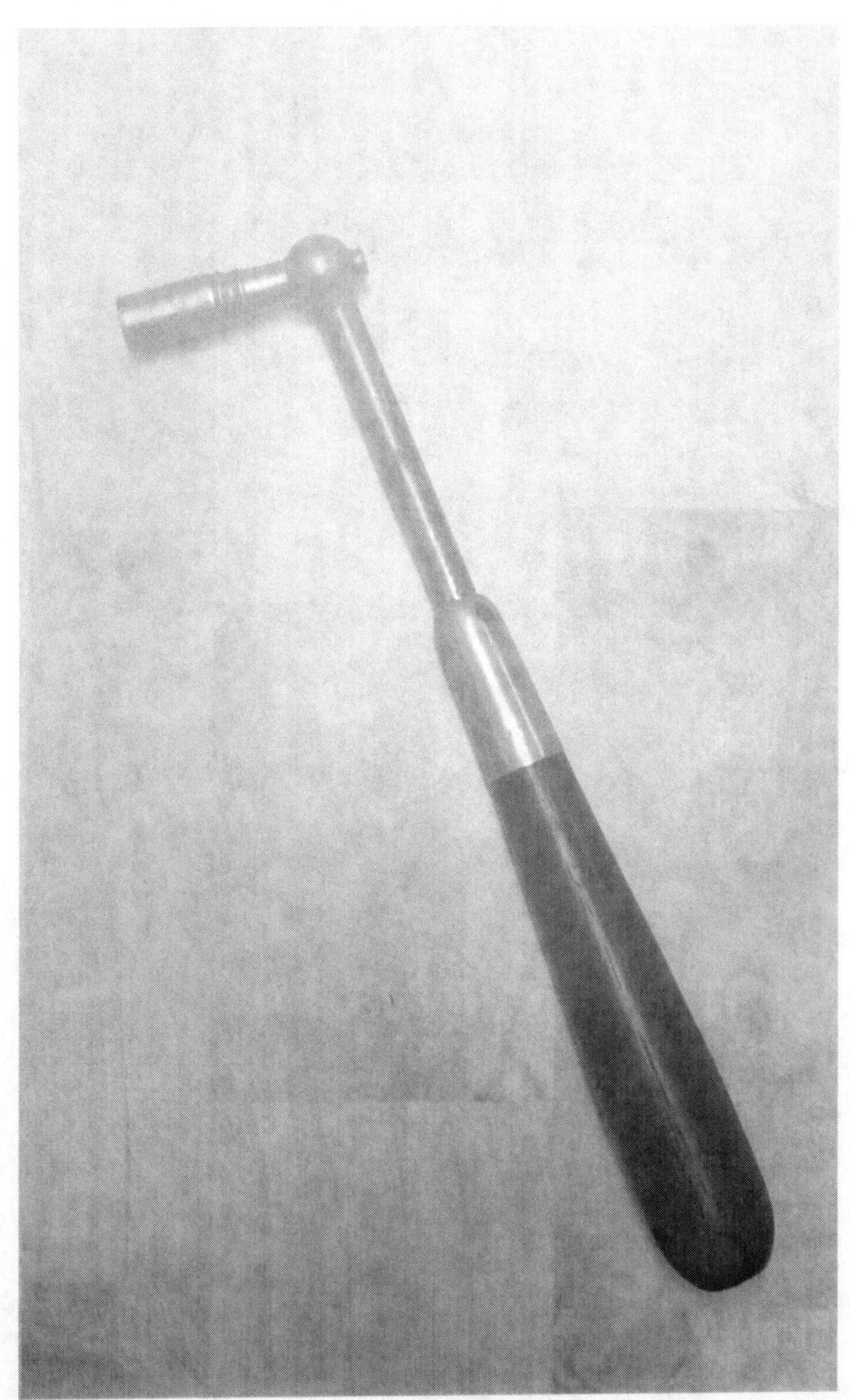

Chapter Thirteen

FINALLY, THE TRUTH

A few days later, when we got home from school, each of the Meanderthallers (except me) had a letter from the mayor waiting for us. Our presence was requested in the Town Hall hall at 4 pm Friday. I learned about the meeting from the Meanderthallers in a Thursday after school chocolate malt session. Maybe mine got misplaced at the post office, or my dad stuck it in his pocket and forgot to give it to me, or...I decided not to ask. I would just show up at the meeting.

Each of us wondered, "What now?" as we trooped into the Town Hall hall, like the seasoned veterans we were becoming. There was a head table and a table for us Meanderthallers with seating for us to face the head table. Extra tables and chairs were scattered toward the back of the hall. Four folding chairs parked against the wall just inside the hall door across from the mayor's office.

We got a fresh bottle of our favorite pop, two napkins and a plate for cookies as we headed for our table. We were sipping, giggling, and generally showing how nervous we were at this formal invitation. Had something new turned up regarding the cause of Frank's death? Then the back tables started to fill with grown-ups. Parents stopped at the coffee table or grabbed a bottle of pop on their way to the back tables. Johnny T, escorting Jim formally to a table just behind the Meanderthal table, held her chair as she sat down. When Johnny T didn't sit next to her, Melvin jumped up and got her a cup of coffee and a cookie. Johnny T had oozed back to join my dad holding up the wall—that's our way of saying they were leaning against the back wall. There were town council persons, store keepers, town folks, and plain nosy people curious about this meeting sitting at the other tables.

We quieted down in a hurry, sat up straight, and took to whispering to each other instead of giggling. The kitchen door opened, and the parade started. First came the state patrolman followed by the sheriff, our policeman, the mayor, Johnnie T, Mr. LaFloy, and finally, Doc Bucky. They had coffee mugs in hand as they found seats at the head table.

The mayor stood up and started the—whatever this was. Quick, I opened my note-taking tablet and licked the tip of my pencil.

"Thank you for coming, particularly the Meanderthallers who have worked so hard to uncover the truth about their friend Frank's death. From the very beginning, they sought knowledge of the truth; was it an accidental fall or murder? We are holding this meeting to share the answer and to share the challenge of how to deal with that answer. Please ask the young men who provided Mr. LaFloy with vital, pertinent information to come in."

Our policeman got up, went to the hall door and opened it. The clang of the jail door reverberated, that's echoed, through the whole building, and in came four of our high school football players, with Ronnie B in the lead. They walked over to the four chairs next to the wall, and sat down. The grown-ups in back started shouting, and we Meanderthallers joined in the racket. I couldn't tell you the words, but the emotions expressed were surprise, denial, anger, and more. The jail door clang, and the appearance of the four guys was somehow connected to the story unfolding, and the mob reacted.

"Quiet down or I'll clear the hall!" Doc Bucky handed the mayor my mother's piano tuning hammer to use as a gavel. "Quiet or I'll clear the hall! And I mean I want it QUIET—NOW." The tuning hammer hit the table with a BANG!

It got quiet.

The Mayor turned to our policeman. "Officer, would you please start this meeting?"

I was stunned at the comfortable authority of our policeman as he rose, walked around the head table, and stood where everyone could see and hear him. This was not the bothersome cop who bugged us with his hovering. The person standing before us was a poised professional, a lawman to be respected. I turned to a fresh page on my note-taking tablet. I wanted a record of this speech.

He opened his mouth and out came words, unbelievable words.

"I am here to offer an apology to the Meanderthallers. From the discovery of Frank's body, they have fed me—er—us clues and observations that we found more convenient to ignore. We all know about Frank's gloves. Mary Clare noticed they were missing right away.

She also noticed his cap was missing. The Meanderthallers kept asking questions and seeking information. They displayed good judgment regarding the pistol, allowing us to trace the goons who failed in their attempt to invade Frank's room at the Komfy Kozy Kave-inn. Those goons have been traced to a tong active in Kansas City.

"Mr. LaFloy with his Pentagon contacts provided Frank with a last name and family history. Johnnie T filled in life experiences that made Frank a valuable, silent, national hero. Lots of clues were collected, but until today, the truth to Frank's death was not known."

More murmurings and whispers caused the mayor to raise his hand, still holding mom's tuning hammer. It got quiet.

"Today, I stand before you with an apology to you, my fellow citizens. As your policeman, it is my sworn duty to protect you, to provide a safe place to share information, and to stand above corruption. Since the incident of the railroad handcart—I believe you Meanderthallers call it the teeter-totter handcart—I have let my fear of my bosses, the town council, and my comfortable job security, corrupt my sworn duty to honesty."

He reached in the paper bag sitting on the head table and pulled out—Little C couldn't get to my braid fast enough—I yelled, "That's Frank's hat!"

"Yes, Mary Clare. This is indeed the hat Frank was wearing the night these four high school athletes took the teeter-totter handcart for a ride. Mr. LaFloy told me about his visits with these four young men. Individually, they tell the same story about being nervous before the game, and convincing themselves beer would provide calm and comfort. They admit to stealing a case of beer from the Terrell Truck Stop.

The crowd began to crank up but stopped as the tuning hammer, still in the mayor's hand, started to rise.

"You all need to know restitution has been paid, and apologies made. Each of the four admits to being blitzed, out of it, drunk as a skunk, and unaware of their surroundings as they teeter-tottered back to town, where they tipped the handcart over rather than put it back in the shed. I was the one who discovered the handcart on its side by the depot. I was the one who retrieved Frank's cap from the front timber rail and saw the splotch of blood here on the hat. I am the one who concealed evidence of—what? These four young men were too drunk to know anything, other than if they kept teeter-tottering, they would get back to town. It is not a murder. There was no intent. There was no premeditation. There is no memory. Circumstantial evidence points to a connection between the handcart and Frank's death.

The crowd silence was deafening.

"Now comes the time for a decision. Do you Meanderthallers, you friends, you families, you town people want to prosecute? Or do we look at the evidence, this circumstantial evidence, and consider this an unfortunate fatal accident?"

The silence in that room was total. Broken finally when a woman in the back of the hall fainted, causing a flurry of activity from the men who picked her off the floor, and the women hand-fanning her until she came to. After a sip of cold water, she sat up, stood up and started to speak.

"That is our oldest son up there. He's a good boy. He works hard to get good grades, and has to give up a lot so he can play football. He's very aware of what alcohol can do to a man. He lost an uncle to drink. He did this dumb stunt trying to be one of the guys. He told his Pa and me what happened after he had a talk with Mr. LaFloy. Please, neighbors, listen to him. Now I'd like him to tell the rest of his story."

Bobby, the tall, whippy, string bean of the four, stood and cleared his throat. "My ma is right. The rest of my story is this." He held up a goldstone heart. "Mr. Frank gave me this, after the Homecoming game, the game where I caught that last-chance pass, in the end zone, on the final play of the game. We won the Homecoming game because of that pass. That night, Mr. Frank waited in the cold and snow until I came out of the locker room. I almost brushed past him in my hurry to get to the homecoming dance. Heck! All he wanted was to tell me he appreciated all my hard work, and hand me this." The goldstone heart twinkled as he held it high. He choked up, started bawling, couldn't say any more, and there stood four guys grabbing Kleenexes out of the box the policeman handed 'em.

Then Ronnie B and the other two guys each made a straight -from-the-shoulder statement of their participation in the stunt. They could hardly get the words out over the remorse felt when they realized they might have hit Frank on the trestle. It was clear they felt guilty as h-e-double-fencepost. Each one told of a personal encounter with Frank, and the inspiration to do their best trying to earn a goldstone heart. That's when Mr. LaFloy stood up and gave a talk I will never forget.

"Here is the perfect opportunity for us church goers to practice what we preach. We missed the opportunity to play Good Samaritan to Frank, but here is a golden opportunity to forgive our brothers. Let's agree to never forget all the 'shoulda, coulda, next-time-we'll...' opportunities we missed. Forgiveness? A word with real meaning on this occasion. These four young men are at a crossroad in life. Can we help them straighten up and live positive lives, or will we be the ones who load on anger, hatred, revenge, and other negative attitudes that will twist their lives forever?"

He turned and looked directly at the four repentant athletes. "Fellas, I challenge you to remember Frank every day of your life. Each of you knows about the goldstone heart award. Check yourself before you go to sleep each night and ask if you earned your 'Frank's heart' that day. Learn about the way of life he called 'no-count giving.'" He turned to Doc Bucky and asked if there was anything he forgot.

Doc grinned and added, "And stick to coffee or soda pop."

The place erupted with cheers and shouts of "It'll preach" and laughter and back patting. Doc Bucky took the tuning hammer away from the mayor before he busted it trying to regain control of the meeting. We Meanderthallers went up to hug Ronnie B and Bobby and the other two guys. They thanked us for hanging in there until the truth came out. I bet they never steal the handcart again, and hopefully they'll stick to soda pop. I bet they, being leaders, preach the lessons learned for the rest of their lives.

All of a sudden I started backing up 'cause someone was pulling my pigtail. Johnny T's voice came from behind me as we stopped in the kitchen. "The old scoundrel says to tell you he's proud of you."

"Huh? Who? What old scoundrel? Where?"

"Your dad, dipstick."

"My dad? Old Scoundrel? Why'd you call him a scoundrel?"

Johnny T had his mouth open to answer when the Meanderthallers gave him the gang rush and pulled us back into the celebration. My brain was on overload so I decided to think through my dad saying he was proud of me first, and then try to remember why the word *scoundrel* kept popping up. For now, surrounded by four very relieved guys, the gang, and a herd of grown-ups, I guess Frank can rest in peace 'cause we Meanderthallers consider this case closed.

Meeting adjourned.

Before I fell asleep that night I remembered I forgot to tell anyone about Frank's cabin—well, now my cabin. And I wondered if we would ever hear from any of Frank's family? Would Johnnie T go back to Texas forever? Who was the guy in camo almost run over by the beer-runners? Why does scoundrel keep coming up? And where was the other half of the goldstone heart? And what is the story behind those seven little rocks? Sounds like there's enough stuff in my notes for at least another book or so.

Would you read it?

LOOK FOR...

TRESTLE
OVER
NO NAME CREEK
The Classroom Edition

CPSIA information can be obtained at www.ICGtesting.com
Printed in the USA
LVOW06s0806280713

345004LV00004B/11/P